Romeo: 'Did my heart love till now...
For I ne'er saw true beauty til this night'

William Shakespeare

First published by Plato Press 2013
Copyright Rebecca Vincenzi 2013
All rights reserved

9798594123199

This is a work of fiction. Any resemblance to actual persons, living or dead, or actual events is purely coincidental.

The Gold Man
By
Keziah Shepherd

For Rehana

I sit here watching the cat. He has big gold ormolu eyes and is still a kitten in his face, with his imagination aroused by the sight of a silk belt, wriggling. He doesn't seem to need true love - I poke him with a stick fondly, and he seems pleased. But it just wasn't enough, physical affection. What I needed was the burning yearning within, fulfilled. This cat doesn't need true love; its instinctive drives are not to be in love. But one day I realized I was different. You're perhaps sceptical, but one day I met 'love at first sight'. I'd read about it before, in Shakespeare, and always thought it something he'd made up. 'Love at first sight': an instant recognition of love - a knowing of love, requiring no effort.

1

When Gerald found a yellow rose hidden in a drawer of our London flat, he suspected I was having an affair. From being disinterested, he begins to wonder what had really happened to me while I was in Barcelona.

"Why is there a yellow rose in the drawer?"

"A man gave me it," I say

"Oh?" he says. He looks interested, as if he was surprised by that.

"What man?"

But I don't speak. I really don't really understand what happened myself. It had been my last evening in Barcelona. The last flecks of the orange, setting sun were disappearing and I had seen the gold statue again. He was standing on a plinth, surrounded by tourists and not only was he handsome, there was something very rich, in his being that anyone might feel cheered up, to get one look from him.

From being so very far away, so very still, he at once, at the sound of a coin's chink, gave off a glow, a flood of character, as something that came alive from stillness: a butterfly from its cocoon.

I peered over someone's shoulders, glad to be hidden from his view by the many spectators, but, something held me, something kept me watching him, and when the people in front of me moved away, I was in full view of him, and if he should move his eyes my way, I knew that he would see me.

I had seen him two days earlier at midday. I had just come out of the covered market and seen him standing on 'Las Ramblas' in the centre of Barcelona: a dazzling gold painted man, stood on his pedestal, motionless. At regular intervals, people were stepping forward, dropping coins into his little box, and he would move, shaking their hand and giving people a warm smile, with his brown eyes.

He was dressed up as a king, or Spanish lord and standing on a cubed pedestal. His skin was painted completely gold and shone like brass and he stood up, proud and still with deep, dark brown eyes behind his gold skin, which were shining. He looked out, as if at a world beyond the people. A small boy stepped forward and dropped a coin into a little box at the foot of the pedestal. There had been a chinking noise and all at once, the gold statue began to move. His arms seemed to melt out of their stiff pose and he began to bend forward to shake the boys' hand like mechanical toy come alive, nodding his head and winking his gold-lidded eyes.

I knew Gerald would never have approved if I dropped a coin. I clearly heard Gerald's voice saying to me "another tourist being ripped off by a local" and I waited where I was, holding my uneaten fruit.

The people had laughed when the boy ran grinning at his mother. As the statue resumed its original, static pose, I felt myself grin as I had done as a little girl seeing a game I liked to play.

I waited eagerly for someone else to drop a coin in his box. 'What could come' I had thought, 'of dropping a coin into the gold man's box too? What was wrong with rewarding this gold man for his creativity and playfulness?'

I felt my fingers search for a coin in my pocket. The urge to drop the coin throbbed and throbbed and I felt myself move to drop in a coin, even with the peoples' eyes on me. I found that my hands searched for my purse full of coins with a will of their own. It seemed they moved of their own accord and then I threw the coin into the box, and looked up at the gold statue with a smile.

But this time, on hearing the chinking noise, when the gold man's eyes flickered alive, his brown eyes watched me, and then, it seemed as if they were struck by a sudden emotion. Their sparkling brownness all at once became intent and serious. Rather than shake my hand, his hands remained by his sides and his eyes simply watched me earnestly. He watched me for a long time and didn't move. In fact it was a long stare, a stare that didn't stop: rude and without cease. I thought that his eyes had become heavy, brown, and almost sorrowful as they watched me, too seriously, as if they'd been reminded of something stony and chill, and of something too serious and so deeply sad, awoken by the sight of me.

Uncomfortable in the stony scrutiny, I stepped back and walked away from him. He continued to watch me as I walked away, having given no handshake, and I felt a thud of fear by his look, as if I had opened a Pandora's box, and now I wanted to get back to my hotel and hide from him so I took the path back to my hotel.

I felt deeply uncomfortable. 'What was that look?' I thought. It was so serious it made me feel afraid. I wanted to get away from it, for it seemed so dangerous a look that I felt vulnerable. He looked like one of those men in love films who had felt something deep and serious and painful. I thought it best to get back to my hotel room and lock myself away, but then, after a while of walking, I began to change my mind, thinking that the idea of anyone loving me at first sight was implausible, for I had pimples, and he couldn't have been serious. The emotion in his eyes was so strong, it had to be a joke because I was barely able to keep Gerald loving me, he who had known me for nine years, and I began to decide that the brown eyes were just a joke. And I finally concluded that the gold man gave a handshake to the men, and for the women, he gave the 'in love look'.

But that evening, two days later, there I was in front of him again, still wondering about the look he'd given me before: that serious look.

I stood there still curious, still curious to know why he had looked at me like that? My heart beat a little, because I was afraid to see his face react again, and I waited, uncertainly, nervously, my face rather puzzled, amid a street of lazy, tired people looking about for something to do, beside drink, beside wander in the breeze.

I waited for the gold man to turn his face, waiting like someone doing an experiment, to see what would happen if he saw me again?

I was all prepared to keep on my route back to the hostel, stopping off to buy a cheese bocadillo for my supper and felt sure he would not to remember me!

But when his face turned my way and his brown eyes fell on me, they found me, and recognized me at once!

His eyes forgot, at once, their other duties, and aimed on me, as I stood there, amongst the crowd, watching him, with such a questioning look. I frowned slightly as if I still hadn't understood why he'd looked at me the day before, and still puzzled, had come back to find out.

At once, he signalled me to go to him, using his head and when I didn't move, he lifted his arm and waved me over, even though someone's coin had fallen, yet it was ignored by the man. His main concern seemed to be me, and his attention was set upon me, keen now, to get me to go to him.

But I was frozen to the spot and simply looked back at him in alarm, self-conscious at once, and warily feeling the glance of the crowd upon me. Their intrigue had spread, to involve me, and in their boredom, they looked at me, to see what my role was going to be in their evening's entertainment.

I began to shuffle backwards, fear on my face, and so the people began to chuckle, for, from his pedestal, the man stepped down, and began to tread his way, over to me, beseeching me to not run away.

"Are you English?" he said. I, as though dumb, nodded, looking afraid, like a deer, startled, in a forest. "Are you here alone?" he said. I didn't answer this question, knowing that an honest answer would render me vulnerable... and perhaps easier for him to seduce, but after worrying, biting my lip, I found my head nodding anyway. "Do you want to go for a drink?" he said. The people were still watching, as if it were all part of the street mime, and therefore their right to watch. I wished they weren't watching. I bit my lip, trying to decide what I should do. I knew I should say 'no'. The people were still, watching too, as if they wanted to know, wanted to know if I was going to be 'easy' to chat up, or if I would refuse his advances. I felt my face go hot, knowing fifty or sixty people waited to hear my reply.

But the idea of a ham sandwich alone was so gloomy an alternative, and, besides, the man had good English, not the broken, boring kind to listen to, but fluency and an ability to communicate. He was intelligent, and I longed to talk to someone.

So I agreed to have a drink with him, nodding my head, still not speaking yet, and went a little nearer to him to wait, as he picked up his box of coins, before leading me to a nearby cafe.

2

"What happened in Barcelona?" Gerald said, when I was back in London.
"Nothing" I answered, shaking my head.
"You haven't been the same since"
"What do you mean?" I say acting as if I was so surprised. When I got back from Barcelona I had been determined to get back and act as if nothing had ever happened. And when he even asked me if we should try having and baby and stop taking the pill, I said that I thought this a good idea.
I managed to make love as if I really enjoyed it.
"Why aren't you listening to a word I'm saying?" he says "and why do you never talk to me, you act as if I'm not even here" he says, "I want to think about the future... children" he says, and glances at me.
I don't know what to say. Sometimes I consider the children in the school playground being my own. The children leap up to me, throw back their faces until they get bleached by sunshine and shout:
'Maria" and hold my thighs and I say
"Hello there! What do you want to be when you grow up, Anstice?"
"A kangaroo" she says.
In Barcelona I only intended on having a quick drink with the Gold Man. The people were dispersing, murmuring, smiling at the two of us, and I wondered, as my face still felt hot, if they were murmuring surprise that I'd agreed to have a drink with a total stranger (and perhaps they were wondering if I were a tart, who did that kind of thing all the time?)

"I've only time for one drink," I told him, "I have to leave at ten" and I looked at him, to see if he'd understood. I didn't want him thinking he'd get sex, and after be disappointed when I'd have to leave, leaving him sore that he'd given up his evening's work on the pedestal, just for a boring conversation, and wasting his money on a drink. But he nodded happily, picking up his box of money, as if nothing were better than to go with me and we sat at a cafe table together, with an umbrella over it, his face was gold as the brass tools by the fireside while people pointed at us, laughing.

I assumed this was just another man, trying his luck for sex. He couldn't surely have loved me, not how I looked, and I assumed he was one of those men who spent their lives being entertained by womanising, like gamblers gamble and alcoholics drink.

Yet I listened with interest to his conversation. He had a rich sounding voice, as voices sound, once the brain and the heart are at one, and he told me his name was Juan Carlos. I listened, as he explained he had family, in Barcelona, but was in fact from Argentina.

I thought myself brave, to sit down with this crumpled, knolled face - coated in gold. No one else would have wanted to be laughed at, to be the centre of a joke, for, around me everyone wore white or pale coloured clothes, and no-one else in the cafe sat with a mime artist painted gold.

"We are going to have to speak very fast" he said, "If you have to go at ten" and laughed.

I was quite sure that he was a wolf, trying to charm me and I expected that soon I would be walking back to my hostel and eating my cheese sandwich.

But despite this, his eyes had mottled green flecks and I liked his personality - I liked the way he chattered, and suddenly I felt glad to be with him, as he was just the right company, a wit, a live wire, a friendly, kind person. He cheered me up, and suddenly I felt enlivened, and flattered, because he had chosen to be with me, and was losing 25 pesetas every sentence he spoke to me!
And he surprised me, for he was in fact, a tennis player, and I acted interested when he told me about the tennis, but I didn't believe he was really one, just someone who was trying to impress me. He mentioned his family name, but I'd never heard of it.
"I've only heard of Bjorn Borg" I shrugged. He told me he'd played around the same time as him. "And do you still play?" I asked, suspecting that he only said he did to show-off, but he nodded, vaguely.
"There's a court here in Barcelona"
"You should always do the thing you love," I said, and he raised his eyebrows and nodded, knowing so.
"But I've no-one to play who is as good as me" he answered, and when he giggled, I noticed he had a gold tooth, on the left of his mouth. "This is my tennis blemish" and he offered me his large hand.
It was a dark, tawny coloured hand, so that when I touched a piece of tough skin at the foot of his thumb, my own skin looked like sheath of white paper. I let my finger trail over the rough skin, then, as if startled, pulled away, looking at him, astonished, and wondering why I was touching the hand of a total stranger. "Have you played at Wimbledon?" I said, quickly. He told me there were other tournaments, but my eyes glazed over a bit, as he explained where they were.
Then a beer arrived, and I looked amazed at it. I had agreed to a small beer and he spoke to the waiter in quick Spanish and as we waited for the drink he had asked me why I was in Barcelona.

I told him about the conference and quickly added that I had a boyfriend, hoping to impress him: for having a boyfriend was rather like a status thing, meaning that I was loved, by someone and not alone and unloved: something that terrified me more than anything.

But he had seemed neither impressed nor affected. He told me he had a daughter and I asked the age.

"Three" he said

"And the mother?" I asked

"She's a friend" he nodded, smiling, and I waited to hear more, but he didn't say anything else, and I was a bit disappointed. I wanted to know if the woman had been rejected, if he'd not loved her anymore, and it puzzled me, that they could be friends, after a love affair. I felt jealous that he had had a friend, as it was so mature, for, in my own experience, love affairs seemed to end in heartbreak and misery. Once, when this man didn't love me, all I felt was a horrible pain, and as soon as he'd gone, the tears that I'd held back, welled up in my eyes, and I could hardly speak. People said 'What's up?' They made me cups of tea, but the tea really didn't make the pain go away. They said, "This will make you feel better" and gave me a cup of tea, but it didn't. Nothing did make me feel better. It lingered, this pain, for weeks and I lost the sparkle in my eye.

The Gold Man seemed to look sad, as he told me about his daughter, and I felt like comforting him and so I said "It's nice to have someone who will always love you" and gave him an assuring smile, even though I was feeling rather sorry for the abandoned daughter, maybe the result of a passing romantic whim. He nodded, brightening.

But when the beer arrived it was a huge glass, perhaps a litre of beer, and I looked at it, rather hurt, because I felt he wanted me to be drunk, and make me easier to be seduced.

"I can't drink all that!" I said, but he just shrugged. A martini arrived for him. "I saw you yesterday" he said   I nodded, and felt glad that he'd remembered, remembered the moment that he stared at me so strangely. It made me feel better, so I picked up the big glass and took a sip. "Yes" I said.

On the table was my journal. I never confessed to people that I wrote, but I liked to throw down the words that came to me and keep them in my secret journal, out of sight and mind. But suddenly the Gold Man glanced at my journal. "What do you write about?" he asked. I went pink, and shrugged, as if the sight of the journal were an embarrassing mole or fart.

"Oh just bits and pieces" I said, screwing up my face and making as if my bag was a bin, in which I flung the journal into.

Then I sat up and looked at him quietly and said "But I'll write about you" and I looked at him, half hoping he might be pleased that he was going to be written about, but instead he looked about him, at the people passing by and his voice was louder.

"Write about women..." he said, pointing at the crowd, so that I looked over, over at all the very pretty women, far prettier than me (and I rather worried, in that moment, that he would notice another one that he would rather pick up instead of me!)

But he began concentrating instead on his own sudden outburst of opinion "Write about how they all wear trousers... how they have lost their femininity" and he looked at me, waiting for a response. Suddenly I rather wondered if I sat with the biggest male chauvinist ever and replied with a quiet voice, in case he might be angered by my opinion:

"Well for years women have been stuck at home, having babies, now they want to have chances men have had" But the man flung his hand at what I'd said   "From one trap to another" he said, and frowned. I sat, looking forward, puzzled. "See how no-one wears dresses?" and I looked over at the women, realising that every single one passed wore trousers. Then I looked at my own bare legs, and wondered if he had spotted me, because he was glad that I was the only one to wear a dress?

"Words are not important, they are just words" he continued, and sat thoughtfully, his eyes looking at me, carrying, it seemed, some deep understanding that I didn't have, at that moment. But I just frowned, for words were very important to me, and he had seemed to shrug them off, maybe because sport was his thing. I didn't want to argue, because we were strangers, and he was entitled to his opinion, but it felt as if he'd put down 'words' and I felt affronted, on their behalf. "Words are just words" he repeated, and I sat, stunned, not really knowing what to say.

I only know that he spoke to me from some other level, some level I hadn't reached before... and I felt afraid to speak, in case he sensed my ignorance of this level, and I didn't want to 'put him off' being with me, as I was rather glad to be with him. He was unlocking doors in my brain and he was intelligent, not intellectual, just intelligent, that I wanted to be with him, attracted to him, even though I couldn't see his face, for I often wondered if his face was old, the gold face paint made him seem wrinkled.

I planned to leave as soon as my drink was half finished. I was looking at the amber liquid half way up in the glass, and knew I should stop drinking it.

But even though I'd had just half the beer, every other moment the man was looking at my eyes and smiling. I was glad to smile, because even though I couldn't think of what to say, I could at least smile, and it kept him happy, so that he would stay with me, but what was strange, was that every time he smiled at me my vagina felt like a chilli was burning it, and I looked out at the street, to look at something else, so that it would stop burning.

My eyes had begun watering and I looked flustered and red faced, self-conscious, afraid that he knew what was happening to me. I couldn't handle this feeling in my vagina, nor could I stop myself looking back at his eyes, which were brown and glowered so much, and such a pleasure, that I didn't notice anything else at all.

He had a smile like a kind priest, and I felt happy, rewarding him with my own smile,

"People love to make eye contact," he said, suddenly. He looked out at the people passing, so I followed his glance, and saw the tourists, in their white cotton clothes, cameras, caps, trudging by, "they walk along the street, live like this, on top of each other, and never make eye contact!" and he looked at me proudly "I help them make eye contact! I think I do a service" and he laughed. I laughed too, impressed by his contentment, but also worried, for he seemed to have found an inner peace and happiness that I had not, and I felt somehow inadequate, and unworthy. Then he leant forward, and with a quieter voice he said "But I would never tell my tennis pupils that this is what I do now!" And I wondered if he had run away to become a mime artist, had had a nervous breakdown and run away. Gerald, my boyfriend, expected me home the next day and I had never had a drink with another man before. I wondered if I would tell him, just to make him a bit jealous? 'A man asked me for a drink' I could say, 'but of course I left afterwards'

But what was strange was that I couldn't move, and suspected the man had hypnotised me. I shuffled, frowning a little, because my vagina was like a lump of blazing coal. It wanted to get up on its own and go somewhere quiet and I was sure it had produced a sort of gravy in my pants.

I had become nervous and could think of nothing to say, and was sure that he would lose interest in me, should he sense my liking him. I liked him rather too much, and hated to like people too much.

"I can do magic too" he said, leaning forward, quietly.

"Will you show me some?" I said, half joking, but he nodded seriously, looking into my eyes, and I felt a flood of warm run through me. His eyes turned to honey gold and suddenly my face went serious and we both looked at one another for a long moment before he spoke, with a flat, hardly audible voice. "Do you want to come back to my hotel room?"

I looked shocked, and looked away from him, without saying anything, as if to let it dawn on me, what he'd asked.

I hadn't had sex with a stranger like this before. Only fifteen minutes had past. I found I liked this man, but I felt hurt, that all he wanted was a quick bit of sex, and I was afraid of that, afraid of catching a disease, of breaking years of fidelity to my boyfriend.

"Where is your hotel?" I asked, curtly.

"My hotel is just there," he said casually, flipping his hand towards the buildings that overlooked the street. He spoke flatly, quietly, almost as if he was losing his voice and he looked at me, patiently waiting, watching me with his brown eyes.

My heart was beating slowly, but drum-like wooden spoon beats.

"Oh" was all I said.

The idea seemed appalling. I had been faithful to Gerald for the last nine years and Gerald was my rock. When I had met Gerald, someone had said:

"He's a real bastard to women," but I had rather liked the idea of this, like a pirate or Don Juan. Back then my life had felt cold and colourless, as though I'd come out of a beautiful, comfortable spell. My voice had started to warble, and I couldn't help saying sorry to people. I believed that I was just an encumbrance.

I went to my bedroom and preferred to sleep, burrowing into my duvet, being a banana, black, soggy and punched inside, because, awake I was depressed, and, I couldn't get a job and ended up licking envelopes as a job. The only human beings in life were the envelope lickers, and they hardly spoke to me, because my voice sounded like a fly's cry and I kept bursting into tears and every day, I was late for work.

Sometimes, alone in my bed, there seemed to be a man, large, dark, and creeping in my bedroom at night. My heart always jumped. I saw it was only a shadow, but then I thought I saw eyes, sinister, peering out, but they were only teacups. At night the wind was slamming on the windowpanes and the frames were loose and I thought they might fly in like paper. I was freezing too, as my only source of heat was the blue flame, that huffed and puffed on the gas stove, and I could hardly pay my bills, and all the time I seemed to be dying like a worn out battery in a man's razor.

Then Gerald had invited me out for dinner and I happily agreed, thinking as well that a good meal would do me good, because I was living off lentils, canned beans... and suddenly a meal, in a real wine bar, with golden lights, was bedazzling.

When he suggested we have port, at his place, I nodded, because I rather wanted to see what port in a real decanter was like.

I slept with him, under a goose feather duvet, that was crisp and clean, and for a 'bastard to women' he surprised me, because he wrapped his arms around me, like a small child protected, and all of a sudden I didn't feel alone!

The vibration of Gerald's voice ran through me and in the morning, when we showered, he washed me with soap. He seemed interested in me, like a beguiling toy, that hadn't yet lost its enchantment, and I wondered how long it would be before he was 'a bastard'. I was surprised to hear from him again, but he rang, rang me again and again. Each time I was pleased, but not ecstatically, but going out with him meant forgetting my empty life.

Now our comfortable Islington flat was a rare, breathing soft place of a flat, with a candlewick bedspread over the bed with a mattress thick as a Victoria Sponge. Our flat reminded me of the inside of a padded cell, within which I led a routine life, the walls protecting me from a chaotic and menacing world outside.

The cream curtains at the window wavered softly, should it be a nice day and the window was open. Outside there was a view of peaceful gardens and inside, gentle under my feet was a thick grey carpet, moss-like, and always the breathing of Gerald. Whether sleeping, reading, cooking, Gerald was always there. At night, deep, black burning buildings loomed in a burnt umber sky and I dreamed my dreams feeling secure that Gerald was at my side and I was sure this life would go on forever, for love with Gerald was something like a soldier endured, a daily gruel but Gerald and I were pretty happy.

But then one day my boss had the idea that I go to Barcelona.

I had been standing in front of her desk, looking ahead of me, trying to look pleased, to be chosen finally, for one of these conferences, but my heart began to feel chilled and fearful, when I realized I would have to go without my boyfriend Gerald, and I stared down, as if suddenly there were poisonous snakes and black widow spiders crawling all over my boss's floor.

"I don't really like being alone" I had said with a whispery voice and was looking at her appealingly.

"There'll be other colleagues when you get there" she had said dismissively. She was a strong woman, who didn't understand fear, who led the team fearlessly, to new vistas... and I trailed cowardly after her, grateful for the leadership. My heart began palpitating and the entire colour had drained from my face.

"I'll need to check with Gerald," I said uncertainly. I felt ashamed at the whimpering way I'd said it, and she blinked. She did not understand the idea of 'needing' a boyfriend.

"I need my staff trained, whether Gerald likes it or not" she said, with a simple clear tone "If it doesn't suit you, maybe you should be looking for another job?" There was a silent moment, where the words tingled and I was struck by the seriousness of the mission and bit my lip.

When I told Gerald that I was going to Barcelona, he looked very doubtful.

"It's dangerous for a young woman travelling alone. Men take advantage. Are you sure you should go?"

I felt afraid. All night I lay awake worrying. Barcelona seemed impossible to get to. It seemed so foolish, suddenly, to be going on my own. I couldn't believe I was doing something so stupid: travelling alone. It was like something impossible, something only strong people could do... not someone like me.

Eventually I got about packing my bag for Barcelona, but then Gerald came in the room.

"Why have you packed that dress?" he asked with suspicion. I was startled, yet I knew it was a daring dress, showing all my legs, and daring was perhaps a foolish way to be, when alone in another country, so I stiffened.

"It might be hot in Barcelona" I said, keeping hold of it, uncertainly "but I'll put it back in the cupboard if you think..."

"You do as you want" he said, and seemed to be in a huff, and left the room, so that I looked after him, all worried, and looked at the dress... worried it would be too dangerous to wear.

When my coach was due to leave from Victoria Station I went to say goodbye to Gerald but he had been really grumpy. I put my arms around him, my big eyes calling for his affection, but he was stiff and cold, and so I ended up holding him, as if he were a float, and I was trying not to drown. His green eyes glanced at me, watching me, fixedly like pin pricks.

"Bye" he murmured, tiredly, as if I were no longer his girlfriend anymore

"I don't want you to leave me?" I said. My arms reached out, but he had turned his back, and was walking away, without even a wave.

Then the red bus swallowed me up in its soft vibration, and swiftly it sleighed its away along the road, as if out of control, leaving Gerald out of my grasp, and soon he was smaller, faraway, a man in just a suit and tie, now too small even to see. I stared at the last speck of him, feeling as if he were falling down an abyss.

"Fares please" said the bus conductor had said, looking at me.

"Victoria please" I tried to say, but my eyes were tired, my face gaunt, and I had a wobbling voice. I couldn't see. I didn't think I would get as far as Victoria, as I sat there with tears in my eyes.

"I think we'll have a bit of music," the coach driver had said calmly as the coach began to set off for the continent. He had enjoyed chattering. He spoke to the people at the front seats, as if they were intimate friends. He seemed like a pleasant man. He often adjusted his side mirror. He had a ring in one of his ears and had grown a thin moustache the colour of dark wheat. He had a dimple in his chin and sometimes, when the traffic flowed; he lifted his foot off the break and crossed his legs. He wore white socks, white as snow and his arms were latched to his steering wheel and tattoos encircled them like ivy. The letters of LOVE were written on his fingers.

Out of the silence, a man's voice came out of the coach speaker. It was soft, low, sensitive male voice, singing with a piano. The piano notes were melodic and some of the passengers murmured along with him, as the music fluttered up and down the scales between stanzas. I looked up at the speaker, and enjoyed hearing the music.
It was a song about love.
I had only ever believed love to be a frivolous idea, written about in literature and songs as self-indulgence and artifice, but at that moment, the sunlight beamed over my face, and I felt a question rise in my mind. I was a pale woman, of twenty-six or twenty seven, with large blue eyes and shoulder length brown hair, drawn back into a ponytail and my skin was smooth, a little blemished with the odd spot, but I had pretty shrimp pink lips which sometimes smiled shyly. I cocked my head curiously, as I considered the music. I wondered if it had been written by the singer, and if he had written a song about love just for the money or if he had really known about love?
Gerald had told me that love was just something that sold Hollywood films. He was in 'adverts', or he convinced people to buy things, for he was convincing, often people changed their thoughts, after he'd spoken to them, and he had convinced me not to believe in love at first sight and had orange nicotine on his finger, and smoked as if he didn't think lung cancer happened to him, and smoked forty, sometimes sixty, a day.
Victoria Station had been like inhaling a cigarette, and the passengers were seated in clean air of the coach as it moved off for Dover.
The young Spanish men on the coach were talking loudly to me.
"Bella, bella" said the young men on the coach as they walked passed me down the coach aisle. Their eyes shone, fixing on me, whistling and tutting.
"Sympathica" another one of them cooed, as if I was a steaming hot meal, floating before them.

"La princesse" a third said, cooing over me. I shrunk into my seat, worrying and sweating. They had noticed me and were talking to me as if I were a delicious meal.

Islington got further and further out of reach and I just felt more and more anxious. I did not believe I could survive 'unknown' places alone.

I kept feeling tempted to get up and tell the driver to stop the coach, but it was an unusually nice morning, for the weather had changed overnight. It was the fourth day of April and the weather was buttery and golden, with blue skies: silky and pure. It seemed that everyone would love London, if it was always so beautiful, because the sunshine dived against the tarmac, splashing the place with it, while the passengers looked out of the window, faces bright with its custard colour, dreamily looking out at the street.

I was cradled by a gentle murmur of conversation. Spring trees were producing lime green leaves, like magicians producing scarves through bunched fingers. Babies in prams leant forward, like racing drivers. Lemon yellow dandelions fist sized, had appeared out of the soils of Camberwell and over the rooftops, in the distance, the tower blocks were collaged against the blue wallpaper paste sky.

The coach entered the labyrinth of South London, bouncing gently over the roads, rocking the passengers into a passive lethargy. The world through the windscreen seemed to have no sound, except for the road digging machines, which rattled away like woodpeckers. We passed through Peckham, past the Crown pub: 'Toby Beer One Pound thirty a pint' read the sign 'Happy Days are here to stay' It cut through the council maisonettes, placed by town planners at various angles and then mounted a hill, to cross over the vast, green misty Blackheath. Then it descended, down to the motorway, where the roofs of houses looked like red mini pyramids, side by side.

"Dog going on the motorway, " said the driver. The passengers looked with interest at a shiny, furred spaniel, which was determined as the cars to make speed, trotting down the motorway. They laughed, and looked back at it, as the coach swooped past
Parallel with the road, there was a train track and the train slithered along it, leaving a trail of tracks, like the slime of a snail. There were bald areas of land now - coloured green. I saw how we entered new territory. There was a lake of daffodils and an oasis of trees, which glinted in the sun, like a paradise – some little gardener's vision come real and some of the trees were so flowering with blossom, they resembled the fur of long-haired hamsters - fluffy and thickly adorned, and sometimes the land changed colour, sometimes, yellow: a field of rape, and a velvet brown; a new ploughed field.
"I can see the sea" the driver called, cheerfully. He sounded like family, like we were all going on holiday together.
The sea was sparkling like a field full of gold chains. The passengers all looked pleased and began shuffling a little, as the coach began to slip through the town of Dover, passing the hotels lined up along the sea front. Above me loomed the cliffs, white as new flour.

When the coach drove onto French soil, there was a vast sky. It was hazy and grey but soaked with sun, which spilt over me, like warm gravy and the land spread so far into the distance without constraints. Nature was growing and spreading and as I watched each tree, each field, thoughts spilled into my head like a river. From my seat in the coach, it felt like I had levitated above the road. I seemed to be rocketing into my head, into that silent space, universe, that it was always too noisy to hear. Other thoughts, interesting thoughts, not the usual biting niggling thoughts... but thoughts about Ann Frank, the girl who wrote a diary in the second world war, the girl who, in a tiny annex, could have written such a lot and let her mind spill out and have acres of thoughts, even with the third Reich, a restrictive force, breathing over her.

For a while everything was calm. I saw the beauty, the fields green as avocados, and the horizon that turned blue, as if it had turned to vapour. Dividing the fields were shimmering curtains of tall trees, all lined up, and their trunks were more like the tendons inside an arm, pulling them selves out of the earth and reaching towards the sky. All of a sudden, black crows, vulture sized, with rat bodies, rose up from their nests in a black cloud. They would dive like moles into holes in the white sky. Trees stood on either side of the road - as if in dark nightclubs with spindly legs, staggering in high-heeled shoes. Birds blinked like large eyelids in the sky. And when I relaxed I felt like walking, silent like this in my head for days. Sometimes the coach driver made me laugh.

"Do you know why there are red and black roofs?" asked the driver. Nobody answered, but looked at him curiously for a moment, pleased to have a friendly driver, because often a coach driver seemed to be distant, in a world of his own, carrying his passengers as if the journey was a duplicate of the last. "To stop the rain getting in of course!" he cried. He looked about him, and seemed pleased with himself. He was glad to see a few smiles.

The road descended a slope and we passed through little hamlets. I saw a child running though a garden, a church looking as though it might inject the sky and a huddle of black and red roofs.

I hurried into the cafeteria to keep ahead of the men at the back of the coach. I took a little bowl and filled it with salad. I was on a vegetable and fruit diet, for according to Gerald, I had over-productive grease glands due to my body's inability to cope with fats and carbohydrates. Spots rose out of my face as painful lumps, but I didn't have time to chew all the grated carrot salad, before everyone began rushing back to the coach.

Then, when I saw the pale, white buildings, the domes, and the towers of Paris. I felt so uneasy. At first they looked like a fairy tale, too distant to threaten me, as yet. The driver opened a window and caught my eye in the mirror and grinned at me. I smiled back at him, and felt more secure, bonded by the flirtation. I had a strange fantasy, that in Paris, I might ask to go with him, to wherever his hotel was, as Paris grew around me.

The apartment buildings and factories grew in size and soon dirty white and grey condominiums and noisy lorries surrounded me. The driver spoke again I could hear the shriek of planes.

"You'll be pleased to know there are no planes landing at Charles de Gaulle Airport above us" the driver muttered, grinning at the passengers in the rear view mirror. A gentle evening sun had made his face turn orange as fruit. "It's fluid, very fluid, unusual for this time of year. I've done many a trip to Paris. Did it the quickest time I've done it in two hours fifty-five minutes - I saw two trucks on the whole journey. You should be able to see the Eiffel Tower - that's if no-one s stolen it" the driver announced. He seemed to speak louder, for the road was noisier. We overtook lorries that smelt of acrid petrol and fumes.
"They're paid twice as much as me. But you ought to hear the debates in the drivers lounge on the ferry. I tell them I carry forty-nine priceless objects. A truck's cargo can be replaced. Coach drivers are the superior driver and they don't pay them enough."
The coach entered a dark tunnel and the engine made a ghostly whine, while the road descended. I looked ahead of me anxiously, as the coach entered a deep, dark cave-like chamber. Around me there were other coaches, parked. Here the coach stopped and the calming buzz of motion ceased. The engine was quiet.
The men started coming down the aisle.
"Where are you staying?" one asked me.
"Where's your boyfriend?" another said.
"He's here" I lied, sweating again, and worrying how I was going to get away, looking about me for an escape route, but there were about seven of them, and they all seemed too interested in me. "He lives in Paris" I added, sweating all over.
The men had surrounded me, like jackals.
"Bella, bella," they waved, licking their lips, as my metro moved off.

3

Then back in London, Gerald found a business card.
"What's this?" he says, holding it out.
It was the business card of the hotel in Barcelona. My mouth felt dry.
"It's the address of a hotel in Barcelona." I had hid the flower and business card in a drawer and thought he would never find it.
"Why is it in this drawer with the yellow rose?" he asked.
He could see my face was blushing.
"It's just a contact address," I said with a shrug, "a useful hotel, in case we go to Barcelona again" But he examines me and I can feel my cheeks are feeling hot.
When the Gold Man had asked me to go to his hotel room I knew it would be unfaithful to Gerald, yet I'd not wanted to keep the man waiting. He was waiting to know if I would agree to come to his bedroom. My sight flickered into me with stroboscopic hectic panic, thinking about Gerald but my vagina was swollen up like a golf ball, and I wanted to say 'no' as I thought about Gerald, but my vagina was swelling up and I felt appalled to say 'no', for, what would I do, the evening alone?
I wondered if slowly I had gone mad? I wondered if I was losing control? The Gold Mime artist was waiting, waiting for me to decide about the hotel room. He watched me, looking at the people in the street. My heart was beating. I had only spoken with him maybe fifteen minutes. The Gold man was waiting. I felt appalled to say 'no', for, what would I do, the evening alone? And why did Gerald deserve me giving up this nice thing?
I kept looking in his face for his eyes and then looked away from him without saying anything before I swallowed and said
"Alright"

Then like on a roller coaster, I could feel myself travel to the unknown space of his hotel room, my thin white hand cupped up in his gentle, large one, with its thick finger and its tough skin. I was ivory pale and soap boned and my eyes were big and still watering. I looked ahead of me, feeling as if I might, any moment, fall off a cliff, wondering if I'd lost all rational control.

His hand was rough, the fingers thick, large, and his dark eyes looked ahead, confidently. We turned off the street and entered a lobby, marble tiled floor, where the receptionist spoke to him in quick Spanish.

"He wants your passport," he said to me. I searched about in my bag, producing the British Crown, gold plaid, now sure evidence I were no street prostitute... but British, respectable. Yet it seemed to me that the receptionist glanced at me in disapproval, yet I didn't care, for all I could feel were a lemonade fizz of excitement, while everyone else were distorted or drowned in bubbles.

We stood in silence in the lift, and rose up to find ourselves on a cool corridor, red carpeted, where a maid pushed a trolley of white folded towels. She said hello to the man, and I glanced at her, as if annoyed, wondering if the maid was another one who'd been in his room, and wondered if he had a born knack for charming women.

He took out his key, and the hotel door opened onto a large room, with a window looking out over a sea of roofs. There was a large bed in the centre, with neat, white crisp sheets.

"It's a big room," I said, stepping inside, and glancing shiftily at the bed.

"It's an ok hotel" he shrugged, going in after me. He watched me, as if interested in what I might do. I hurried away from him and stood by the window, to look at the embroidered quilt of roofs.

"You have a view!"

"Not much of a view" he said, smiling, but I shook my head and said

"I have no view at all" and told him about the dark courtyard of my hostel and he asked me how much I paid. He seemed impressed by the price, and then he said "But money is not important" I smiled, and nodded, as if that was my philosophy too, but then I noticed all the piles of peseta coins, stacked up on the dressing table.
"But you have a lot of money" I said
"I have to take them to the bank. They're very heavy," he laughed and I felt delighted, as if this job enchanted me. I knelt down to touch them, and then noticed a gold robot mask.
"And what's this?"
"Some days I do a robot, some days I do a statue"
The dressing table was covered in aerosol cans full of gold spray paint, and tubes of gold greasepaint. It looked more like a theatre dressing room, and I seemed to forget the purpose of coming to the room, interested instead, by the mime. I looked behind me and saw a wardrobe, and suddenly said
"There is your tennis racket!" and went over to touch that too. He casually came over and took the racket out of it black padded case, so that I could put my fingers on the criss-cross strings. I was delighted to find it, to find that he really did love tennis, that he'd told me the truth. I could feel him looking at me, and I tried to keep my eyes from looking in his eyes, so I walked quickly across the room, for I could see a door, and I opened it and walked into a bathroom. "You have soap!" I called, taking up the little packets of soap, and looking in wonder at the packaging. I carried it out and held it up to him. "I don't have soap in mine" I said, and looked at him, to find him walking over to the bed.
He had sat down on his bed and was taking off his shoes. My voice seemed to weaken.

"You're lucky, " I said, going to put the soap back down on the sink. I stood for a moment, looking at the soap, before going back slowly to stand in the doorway of the bathroom. From there I watched him, and saw that he'd begun to take off his gold trousers.

The bed had crisp, new white sheets, turned back, invitingly. The maid must have just made it. I looked at the large mirror, on the cupboard, which reflected the bed. I was troubled, did he rent this room just so he could watch the sex, in the mirror? I looked distrustfully towards the mirror. Sometimes men just looking at me and fancying me, made me putty. I looked troubled, worried, but then found that the gold man looked at me. He smiled at me. We kept smiling into each other's eyes. I found myself sitting beside him on the bed.

His legs were muscular, dark Demerara sugar, and I could see his lifetime of tennis had done him good. When he took off his shirt, I saw he had a chest of dark, black hair, but his skin on his arms and shoulders was creamy soft, dark. Now all that he had was the gold face paint. I wondered what his face looked like, and what age he was, whether he was fifty or forty.

"Do you want me to wash off the gold?" he asked, gently. Half of me felt my heart was on fire, and I could not stop smiling into his eyes.

"No" I said weakly. I put my hands on my knees, and waited half worrying that I had gone mad; that loneliness had gone to my head and I was doing the craziest thing I had ever done in my life.

In Paris I had met two men. I had been staying in a hotel on the rue Verrerie and had felt so hungry.

The back window was facing a gully and I could smell bad drains, and on the other side there was a window, flooding with pink light from the streetlamps outside. On the bed was a roll of wadding, I assumed was a pillow but more like a rolling pin, and I wondered it would help me sleep. The water pipes sounded like gas, every time someone upstairs washed. Below I could hear scooters bleating and voices of men talking.

The lobby of the hotel had been brightly lit, smelling of fresh bread and sweet chocolate and I peered timidly over at a man, who sat behind the desk, still as a clock, on a mantelpiece.

"How long are you staying?" the man had asked me, peering at me over the counter.

"Just tonight," I said, hardly audible. I signed my name in the hotel logbook, looking at him suspiciously, for would he realise that I was alone, and take advantage, breaking into my room at night, to rape me?

"I'll give you an early morning call" he said. I had nodded, smiling at first, but as soon as I was in the lift, I wasn't certain, wasn't certain that I really wanted him coming up to my room and knocking on the door? I was afraid he might be licking his lips, like a wolf, that it was rare to have women staying on their own, in hotels...

But then I was hungry and lonely. I decided to creep out of the hotel unseen and find a phone box on the street corner. I got quickly inside the box and dialled the numbers for Gerald but the phone just rang and rang and there was no answer. I put down the receiver and felt blocked and trapped.

When I came out there was a group of men lingering in the street. The men surrounded me, and began to smile, as if I were a delicious sight.

"Mademoiselle" they said "let us buy you a drink!" I looked around for a way through, frowning. "Je ne comprends pas" I said, slipping by them. But they called for me again, holding up their arms, protesting. I hurried away, terrified, missing Gerald's presence, for; these men never went near me, if he was there. I felt like a rabbit or a fox, having a pack of dogs after me. The streets were not a peaceful, Paris street, but a war field, spears aimed at me, from all directions.

I hurried along the adjacent street and found a blackboard sign upon which was written: "Menu à 50 francs" Quickly I went inside and was greeted by a waiter with big spaniel eyes. There was a vague scent of French fries and behind the little bar was a stuffed duck on the dresser and a man with a black pointed beard, who was getting sozzled at the bar, moving a cigarette to his mouth in slow motion, focussing on me with wet brown eyes, like beef bourguignon sauce.

"Table pour un person?" I asked the waiter. He nodded and I sat in the corner of the restaurant and suddenly I felt very safe and anonymous.

At first I felt a measure of peace in there. There was a faint perfume of wine, and cigarettes and hearing the kitchen hissing. There was American blues being played and the waiter was striding around, eying plates with the tenderness of a lion her cubs and whisking them away safely before anyone could notice. There was a chandelier - like a gas lamp, with flame light bulbs around it hanging on four chains over the bar - and a goldfish bowl - with a gold fish the diameter of the bowl, with an orange fan tail, swimming around. There were glasses, sparkling like a town at night, perched upside down. I happily chewed to a pulp the ham, rillettes and smoked sausage, mopped up with bread.

But then I began to feel lonely. Sometimes people came in, kissing in that French way, and I was longingly wishing it was Gerald coming in, to kiss me, and sit with me. Then, as if to fill my emptiness, I heard the waiter's voice:

"Do you mind if I sit these gentlemen with you?" and I flinched in alarm and saw two men with him. My heart began to beat. I watched with reluctance as the two men sat beside me and thought for sure that they would try and seduce me, and then rape me. Gerald would say,
"I told you so, I told you it was foolish to go on your own"
The men were far younger than I, students, with fresh pink cheeks and the bright flash of their dreams still in their eyes. They leant towards each other and spoke in very quick French. I noticed that one of them had round glasses, and looked like the more serious one, whereas the other had longish brown hair and tawny skin and handsome dark eyes.

I began to wonder if the waiter wanted to pair us up? That he realized my loneliness? That he was giving these men a chance to chat me up? But this seemed just my imagination. 'Bullshit' I said to myself 'why would he want to do that?' and told myself I was dreaming things up again.

So I ignored the men and continued eating. The waiter brought me a small pichet of red wine and soon, after two glasses, I crunched into the crispy French bread, and beyond the munching sound in my jaws, I heard the mumble of peoples' voice, vowels and consonants making unknown sounds.

I ate the pork with chips (crisp, almost like thin ice around each chip) and the pichet of wine was almost gone, to sooth my emptiness. It tasted like it had been soaked in a mahogany barrel - rich thick grapes - red as a sunset, and I thought how it affected my brain too much, for one glass and I lost my focus and now, my lips were floppy, like the man at the bar, with the goat beard and oily black hair, smeared to his head had eyes that were dollops of blackcurrant jam.

But then I heard a voice:
"Would you like some wine?" one of the men suddenly said. They were both looking at me and I looked at my glass. My pichet was indeed empty and I faltered.

Suddenly the men began telling me happily about themselves. They'd led interesting lives, fearlessly, the man with the long brown hair was a theatre designer on the Champs Elysées, and round glasses, the serious one, was a furniture designer and proudly told me he'd won a competition designing a lamp.

I took a gulp from the full glass they had filled, and began to feel more drowsy, more relaxed. They looked at me with glittering eyes so that I shuffled uncomfortably. They were only about twenty-two and ignorant of worries and problems like my own. I kept my own age a secret, for I felt old, ashamed of my age, as if I had lived a long time and not done anything interesting, because I was afraid, and died slowly within it, eaten up by fear. Suddenly one of the men leant forward and said to me:

"Vous êtes tres sympatique sans maquillage" and I was surprised. Gerald never said that. My face was blotched with pimples, and he often told me so, and wished I would get rid of them, but people said it was a nervous rash, and the more he complained about them, the redder they became, making my life a misery.

"Really?" I said, flushing in surprise.

"Do you have a boyfriend?" the serious one asked suddenly. The two men went still, watching me closely. I nodded, pleased, for I did not want them to think nobody loved me, that I was alone and unloved. "But why isn't he with you?" brown eyes asked. "Aren't you in love with him?" he continued. The woman on the table beside them looked at me, as if she too waited for the answer. She screwed up her mouth and poked a cigarette into it. It seemed at that moment that everyone went quiet, the whole restaurant, in that moment was waiting to learn of my response.

"Of course I'm in love with him" I said, nodding, as if the question were hardly worth asking, but there was something flat, something uncertain, in my answer.

When Gerald and I fought, he was so displeased with me that I sometimes hated him. If I stayed too long in bed he would show me the clock, and I would keep my eyes closed.

"Look at the time" he'd say, and I'd ignore him. "Look at the time" he repeated, pulling my arm, and I pulled it off him, getting hysterical, "get off me" I shrieked, and then I would tantrum, hysterical, until he had to slap my across the face, so that I went still and looked at him in the eye with big shocked eyes. For a minute I was dizzy and dazed, and my cheek stung. And then I just got out of bed, like a robot, and got dressed, in any old clothes, I found on the floor, and went to work, wondering why I had been given feelings ... if all I were born to do was just to lick envelopes.

After work I wondered when he'd be home, and sometimes worried that he might be a 'bastard to women', and leave me. I assumed there were other women, in his office, far more attractive then me, with far more interesting jobs... women who perhaps 'thought' during their day, rather than licked. I hardly dared tell him how much I licked. I told him I did administration and sometimes I worried my brain might stop working, because of the licking.

And I considered our drinking: when we drank too much we began to row. The first row, was when he smashed something, I thought it would be the last row. But it was the first. There was a lot of smashing and many rows, and the first of many cracks in the wall, the first of a lot of shouting, a lot of spitting, of sobbing, of pushing, and every time I thought it was the last time, but after the years went by, then I wondered if things would ever change. Gerald's eyes seemed to be fierce when he came home from work, searching me out. I would camouflage myself in the settee; while he bashed bottles with his shoes, shouting at me, about something wrong, wrong with me, with the flat, with life.... it was wrong.

People said I should leave him, and sometimes I did leave him but half way down the road, I began to get a panic attack and I remembered how lonely I'd been... I preferred to have him spit at my face, until four in the morning, than be alone.

Leaving him was something impossible, something only strong people could do... not someone like me. "I can't live alone" I told myself "otherwise I go strange in the head" but I often wondered if anyone would ever love me as much as I wanted to be loved, or if I would be forgotten by love, like an abandoned cabin on a mountain.

But I didn't tell the two men all this, in case it spoiled the image they had of me, where I was feeling very flattered, to have their attention, as if I might be worthy of their attention!

"Want to come with us to a jazz club?" the other asked suddenly.

I considered this. I was familiar with such an invitation. It was the usual invitation where they probably hoped I'd be drunk at the jazz club and easy to sleep with.

So I refused their offer.

Then they tried another way:

"Let us get your bill"

"No!" I answered.

I tried to reach for my bill, but just as my hand touched the saucer, brown eyes snatched up the bill, a thin piece of paper, and held it up in the air. I lifted my hand to reach it, but he held it even higher and shook his head.

"No, no. You're not paying. I am going to pay for you" and he smiled, pleased with himself.

"But I can't come with you to the jazz club" I cried. "I have to leave" I wanted them to know that they would get nothing from me, that they would get no return. I picked up my bag and my coat to prove to them that I was leaving: that I was not drunk or an easy lay.

"No, no. You're not paying. I am going to pay for you" he continued to insist, smiling, pleased with himself. He spoke so calmly, gentlemanly. There was something of the goodness of a monk in his smile. I looked at him in wonder, for a man, never, had done that, not any, bought me a meal, expecting nothing in return.

I stood up, but even when I was trying to get the bill, he held onto it tightly. I looked at him helplessly.

"I have to go," I repeated.

The two men watched me walking out, all at once quiet and a bit sad, smiling after me, as if I were worth being sad about losing! I couldn't, for a long while, believe it had happened, them paying for the meal and wanting nothing in return. I didn't believe there were people who did that? Wasn't it always to get something or someone?

I walked back to my hotel in wonder as the moon above glowed moth white, and the air was silvery and still. I looked up at the high apartments - with their shutters - their wrought iron balconies and long French windows, and a strange fantasy entered my mind: a warm, glowing room with a lover, making love - then seeing the sky over the golden sandstone buildings and the next morning I woke up, had breakfast and found myself wandering the streets of Paris with a different point of view.

The hotel receptionist seemed kinder.

"Your early morning call. C'est huit heures" he'd said in the phone. Running straight into the shower, it had powerful spiky spurts of water, which whipped my skin like wire and I rubbed myself over in medicated shampoo, using every big crisp towel there was.

The man sighed a lot when he walked - as though it was a hard world, walking from his comfy chair to his desk, with sweeping brush hair, puffy cheeks and tender, rather swollen brown eyes and I followed him nervously down some stairs, as he lurched from side to side 'en bas', but once downstairs, I regretted it, for there were no windows and it was silent. All the chairs were on the tables and I could smell disinfectant, but that smell when it's been put on with a smelly old mop. However the croissant was crisp and buttery and when he asked
"Ca va?" I smiled and used some school French
"Les croissants sont delicieuses" to which the man looked encouraged and said "Voudriez vous un autre?" I considered this, but my belly was jammed full, and I worried the breakfast was manure for tomorrow's crop of spots (especially after the chips I'd had) and already I could feel a livid red one coming up on my chin.
At the back of the Hotel de Ville it was golden and I thought it was perfect walking in the sun, because it touched me all over and soothed me, making me stop, forget worries, like a tranquilizer. It made me gaze over the wall at the river Seine, which seemed to snooze and drift, and sometimes its current looked all twitching, like rice water, simmering, to watch the blossom trees flirt, tossing around their pretty pink lashes and curls and frills see St Germaine church, the Louvre.
At Gare du Lyons I went to the departures screen, and held back my head, to see the list of cities 'Roma', 'Monte Carlo', 'Biarritz', 'Venetia' Mine was a long, grey coloured train, so very dusty and dirty, that I could hardly see inside, but I could see cream upholstery, and when I climbed inside, I saw the seats were shiny, wide, not the thin carpeted seats of northern Europe, and that there were just a few passengers, no groups of men, to my relief.

I watched how my companions on the train also had gentle, calm faces. They calmly watched the apartment buildings pass by, with their sandstone walls, balconies, shutters, The voices in the carriage: Spanish, French, were jabbering their stories, all around me. They watched the land pass by, seeing it sway in the jelly wind, tinged with a gold powdering of sunlight. The spring trees could be seen, and soon the train arrived in the countryside, and the land passed, its winter beaten self slowly springing its way out, in forms of green and delicate colours.

On the left the bony trees stood in a corridor, with skinny trunks, flickering as the train passed, like a herd of nervous roe deer, running away in the evening sun. There were waterfalls of pink sand, dripping over the hillside of firs and silver birch trees. Some of the birches were all in rows, like a hall of mirrors - endless rows, their silver barks flashing and glittering in the whiskey coloured sunlight. People in the farms, rooted like buttercups to the soil, tending to the cows whose mouths hovered closely to the grass and the village people wearing lose buttoned shirts, and after watching, I began to lose count of time and space.

But I was unable to let my stiffened, wiry body relax. The seat had weary springs under the padding yet it was blancmange-like and uncomfortable, and I waited, hoping soon that the train would set off. The train began to move, the hinges and springs and chassis of the train began to make noises, altogether, like a jumbled up orchestra: groans, moans, squeaks and gratings.

My own voice rested in my throat, ill at ease, unused to being still for such a long period. It wanted to bleat, to moan, to cry. Sometimes I felt strangled, panicked - knowing I wouldn't be able to sob in anyone's ears should I need to.

The train seemed to scream, grating along the tracks, as if it had a nightmare and I stared at the flash of the train tracks, feeling the pulse of my heart as I tried to keep calm and then, found the toilet. No one had picked up the toilet seat to piss. There was no more tacky pink toilet paper - the stuff on the floor I wouldn't risk rubbing upon my sensitive vagina - a wound, a chasm of watermelon flesh - too precious to infect. As I returned to my seat, I thought that I must have had every man's urine in the train carriage on my thighs. I passed their sleepy eyes, which glanced at my movement, and wondered if they knew I had a part of their liquid sticky on the back of my thighs.

My book was about a puppet. Its eyes were mirrors. If you looked at his face you saw yourself. In everything you saw yourself. It was your own story.

The book was about children who were born wonderful and aged and rotted if they didn't find the true thing in life: that is to know oneself and love oneself, loving who you were supposed to love, without letting anyone prevent it.

The train was passing the palace of Avignon where I had once scraped 'I love Gerald' into the wall, and deep in the south. The houses were like whole packs of butter hatted with red prism roofs. In the distance were two Renaissance palaces, as if from a Leonardo Di Vinci painting, defying the look of the 20th century.

The houses were now warped in the heat, tiled roofs and the tiles were peach pink and mostly the shutters were closed, as the sun was beating down on them. It looked warm; the trees were thick with leaves. I looked out at the blinding landscape, where the barns had ragged edged wooden doors, where the leaves fluttered like butterflies and the grasses were as soft as the hair above someone's lip, and more and more, the engine sounded like a fierce shower or waterfall.

And then a man sat down in the seat opposite. His eyes were almost black as olives and he had a black bristled chin and soft lips. His lips were pink, and met in the middle tenderly, like two pieces of lychee fruit. I never once took my feet off my bag. I wanted to move, to change seats, but would it be worse where I went? Would there be another man there?

I tried ignoring the man but couldn't help feeling a constant anxiety about his presence. I tried to be distracted by the field of mocha brown goats running to flee the waddings of wind which unfolded over the mountain sides scabbed with green terrain and rock, cut away like gingerbread but I kept feeling threatened that he sat there. It was hotter outside now, and sometimes, when the train slowed down, just over the engine, I heard the crickets sound like broken twigs. I saw the rusty soil, the Cyprus trees, like pen quills, writing on the corrugated fields, and the grape vines, hills of them, with little sticks to hold them straight. The train passed through the fields of yellow rape, the new ploughed soil the colour of pizza bread, stretching out, with the horizon turning silver, but zigzagged with Cyprus trees, or speckled and bumpy with olive trees and emerald green bushes and trees.

Then the man finally spoke. I jumped:

"Is it Montpelier you want?" he'd said, clearing his throat slightly. I turned to look at him, as he hovered forward a little.

"Pardon?" I said. He flinched for he could feel my eyebrows descend, annoyed.

"The train separates there... half continues to Barcelona the other half up to Montpelier." I raised my eyes, surprised. Looking out, I felt a sense of guilt. I had misjudged him. He was just being kind.

"Are we on the right side for Barcelona?" I asked anxiously.

"Yes" he smiled. I breathed a sigh of relief.

Now the rocks were like crumble on apple crumble and the yellow flowers were blooming on the maquis, amongst the heather. The train passed the Mediterranean, which was blue and green, like a lot of large eyes, flecked with white eyebrows and a pink town grew on my left, a lot of golden cubes, sprinkled on a slope that lead down to the still blue sea. The grass was so new, squeaky green and old men came out of their farms, looking at the bright sun, with short sleeve shirts, shuffling frailly with shocked eyes as if they'd just walked out of an earthquake. The churches had crosses, that seemed to be made out of black lace, and were painted with shrimp pink, white or yellow, and the sun shone over them, like a spotlight.

I watched the flamingos, as the train travelled through the Camargue, and saw a sheet of silver, speckled with the pink creatures. There were also ostriches, with sack of potato bodies, and long stick legs, farmfuls of them, turning their pip size heads, to look at the train, as it passed. Then I saw the horses, lying on their sides in the green wigged fields, chestnut horses, shiny as conkers with manes and tails swaying like underwater seaweed.

Finally a dense settlement appeared, and I could make out red and grey roofs, and a whole clutter of sand coloured walls within the silver mist of a city. Large advertising photos began to stand by the side of the track, names of shops, of supermarkets.

"Barcelona?" I asked the man.

"Yes," he nodded. Both sides of the train were now crowded in tall buildings, weaving roadways busy with traffic and pale concrete tower blocks. The train was slowing down and I looked out of the window at the noisy station.

Soon the man stood up, and reached to the rack above, to take his coat, and I watched him leave me as the brakes fell still with a last whimper.

"Good luck. I hope you enjoy Barcelona," the man said simply.

"Thank you" I nodded.

4

"What did you do then, in Barcelona?" Gerald asked.
"Nothing, really nothing at all" I said, "I realised how much I love you" I say... how lucky I am to have found you"
"Well you don't act like it," he said. I swallowed. He looked suspicious. "So you've nearly got rid of me," he says while putting on this cream blue shirt, new from the plastic dry-cleaners packet, unable to get ready if I'm up when both of us are furrowing for clothes at the same time, moving side to side to get mirror space.
I thought of the mirror in the Gold Man's bedroom. He had been wearing a pair of smoky blue boxer shorts. His back was shiny and smooth and he glanced at me looking at it with interest, curiously. I watched his eyes come closer to me, looking at me with the sad and yearning eyes, just as he'd done in the street. I was frozen, by his side, like a block of ice, but felt him put his lips on mine, and be touched by him, a stranger and my lips were shocked, their skin only touched by Gerald, but I continued, interested by his melting gold honey eyes.

He kissed me lightly a while before lifting off my dress. His hands were rough and I felt them surf over my skin, and so I did the same, feeling the warm of his creamy skin, and feeling how large his body was, the mounds of the muscles, the silkiness of the hairs, seeing the black, grassy chest with wondrous eyes and when I let my hand stroke the hairs on his thighs I saw that his eyes oozed with a shy pleasure and he touched my face. I looked down, shy in his gaze. I was glad that Gerald had made me buy some new underwear, because it looked clean and white, and I caught a glimpse of it, in the mirror, as I stole for cover under the white sheet.

Then our legs burrowed their way into the cool interior of the bed. We were lying side by side and I looked at his caramel coloured skin and the thick hair of his chest, before he rolled onto me. He hardly squashed me, or smothered me, but was just on me and I felt the stiff penis pressing into me and he was kissing different parts of me, even under my armpits (even though I hadn't showered) and around my breasts. The kisses were light, leaving petal soft traces, like he was covering me with flowers and his large fingers searched about my body.

I lay, watching his mouth kissing my stomach. I knew he was on his way down to my navel, and down there, he began to lift off my knickers. I frowned faintly, as I didn't really like men going down there, but he didn't see it, for as the cold air washed against my vagina, I blushed and frowned, wishing he hadn't put his face on such private a part of me, but he didn't seem to mind the smell, rather he was letting out a long hissing breath. I felt it echo, deeply inside me, as if I myself had breathed like that, and tears welled in my eyes.

Suddenly I felt a wriggling wet thing, like a panicked little fish, flapping about amid my vagina and I knew it was his tongue, tasting me, and I wished he wasn't, it felt odd, a stranger's head, between my legs, giving me wet licks, and I put my fingers on his head, and stroked his black hair, turning to look in the mirror. I saw that the sheet had slipped off and my body looked milky but rather ill at ease; yet a year of swimming had done me good. Then he lifted his head. His face was all wet and around his mouth, pinky coloured, and he looked like he'd been asleep, and he came up to kiss me on the mouth and that was when I saw the penis.

I recoiled to see another penis. For nine years I was so used to Gerald, and this one had grown, large, and the colour of chorizo sausage, and I felt alarm, because it was so big, bigger than Gerald's and was sure it wouldn't fit in me, and I was worried I would be filled with danger, disease and my voice blurted out, with a squeak "Do you have a condom?" I curled up, like a baby in a womb, listening for the crackling noise of paper being torn, and then felt him come beside me again, making a ditch of mattress, so I tumbled near to him. Calmly he was stretching the rubber thing over his penis, and then there was a small bauble, like an air bubble at the top of his penis, and satisfied, he put my legs on either side of him and made as if a mole, ready to burrow. My skin was pained, as he pushed in the penis, but then my skin seemed weepingly pleased, oiling its route into me and once he was happily installed he began to murmur in Spanish and I was rocked to and fro, listening to the words, which breathed over my face and into my ear lobe, and made me wonder what he said.

I closed my eyes, wondered if he was talking to his wife, the mother of his child, who was in Buenos Aires, far away, and he missed her... or was he saying how beautiful I was? The words sounded like a prayer, whispery, and I thought how much it sounded like someone murmuring in a church, in the confessional box, yet here I was, in this hotel room, with the rustling white sheets about me and the evening sun barely marking the walls yellow. Sometimes he licked out my ear, and I worried there might be wax, and I was relieved that his head hovered above me, all the time skimming over my tummy and rearing back again, making my eyes water each time

"We could come together" he said "is better" So I closed my eyes, to try and concentrate, make myself come, but I knew I wouldn't, the shyness numbed me and instead I placed my hands on his back, enjoying to feel the rubberiness of his flesh, and the smoothness and the warmth, kissing the sides of his face. I felt the prod of his penis, trampoline within me, and felt it pleasant, but his head was moist, and sometimes beads of wet sweat dropped on me, and I held his damp body, while he was muttering in panic, as if he were falling. I wondered if the people in the neighbouring rooms could hear the noise we were making. "Cum, cum" he said, as if impatient. "Is better to come together" I looked worried, and tried, but then looked as if I'd failed.

"I can only come using my finger," I said, biting my lip, even though it wasn't the truth, but I was afraid. I didn't want to hurt his feelings, and feel as if he'd failed. Then he groaned like a puppy, and fell still, in my arms, and after a few seconds of stillness, he laid back, his head on the pillow. I put my head on his hairy chest, and felt the soft black hairs of his chest tickle my nose. I imagined my dad meeting him and imagined us falling in love.

Now his penis was flaccid, reminding me of a cooked sausage, loose in its skin "Is all in the brain," he said. I nodded; glad he thought it my fault.

I listened to his breathing through his ribs and began thinking I had better get out quickly and pictured going back down in the lift, out the lobby and onto Las Ramblas again. But it felt so strange to be feeling so contented, laying on his chest with a total stranger, who'd brought me up for sex. Did he like my snuggling up to him? I felt scared again, that I felt so attached, to a stranger, and as soon as I had lay for maybe twenty of so seconds I sat up.
"I'd better go now"
Picking up my pants, I put them on; searching for the right side of my dress, for it was inside out. I didn't look at him, mainly because I wanted to hide my feelings and decided it was time to go. I wanted this happy moment to last on a good note, without any pain and unpleasantness.
He blinked, without speaking, watching me. I had noticed that he had sat up too, a little surprised and watched me as I scrambled my way into the dress, and was grabbing my bag, before pausing to look at him and wish him goodbye.
"Well, goodbye then" I said, nodding. The gold man pondered me, as if uncertain of me, before saying.
"Hadn't you better wash off the gold first?" Surprised, I looked over at myself in the mirror to find my pale face was smutted all over with gold, and now, glinting, I was a gold statue too. I smiled at him.
"Oh" I said.
In the beginning the city had seemed like a menacing city: a bulls-eye of crime and aggressive men and I didn't want anyone to think I was vulnerable and lost. The cars zoomed by, the lorries shrieked like Dracula and I worried that I was being beeped at because I was a female tourist. All the local women were bronzed and black haired and walked about with easy bronzed limbs and not a drop of sweat on them. No-one else had my colour hair: my pale ash brown colour, and a skin, so ghostly pale, so spotty and greasy - so freakish to look at. I felt out of place, among these bronze beings, so confident in sun.

I crossed green grass lawns and statues but the evening sun was blinding, and my eyes were scrunched up. I tried to act as if I were a local, but, wearing my cardigan and coat, I looked like a stuffed corn dolly, all bundled up, and my face was drenched in sweat. The rucksack weighed on my back, and my hair stuck to my forehead. I strode down a busy road, looking in wonder at the central reservation, which had huge tropical palm trees growing from it, appearing out of the earth like melted corns, and their trunks concertinas of gnarled bark.

Then I smelt sea salt, exhaust fumes and the sea's salty wind breathed down my back and sizzled upon the sweat that burnt in the sun. As well as the boats, the harbour was a lot of rope, knots, poles and floating metal. There were giant palace-like buildings, looking over the harbour, with rectangle, balconied windows, globes and triangular fronts. I walked before them; keen to get my map out, but afraid to. Men sleeked by me, and I thought they would chat me up - and I felt weary when they looked at me. Two of them passed and sniggered, but I wanted no-one to see me. I looked like a nervous wreck. The sun made my head ache. With my hair like a beacon, drawing attention to me, I felt weak, and I was hungry and I felt I was about to faint. I heard more beeps from cars, and cries:

"Sinorita" and the blazing sun made the sweat pour down my face I staggered, the rucksack weighing down on my back, and felt dizzy. Everything went white and I wondered if I was going to be able to stay standing, or if I was going to drop on the floor.

Going up a narrow alley, I came to a cool patch of shadow, made by the parade of shops facing the harbour and navigated my way through a labyrinth of narrow lanes, where an old man with a golf ball chin, sold Mickey Mouse balloons and a barber shop was full of men with neat, black moustaches, having their hair cut.

I crossed Placa Reale, a shabby old square with three dying palm trees that were reaching for the sky like tarantulas, where three drunks stared ahead smiling as if there was a clown show happening, and came to the front of a hostel.

On ringing the doorbell, the door sprang ajar. I went up a flight of stairs and there stood a man with an orange face and a soft smile.

"Signor - do you have a room?" I asked him. The man seemed startled by my high voice, for its anxiety disturbed the quiet peace.

"Yes" he answered kindly, and smiled at me, as if he'd been expecting me and was glad to harbour me. "This is the quiet season" and he gestured for me to follow him. He led me to a room at the end of a dark corridor. "It's just right, thanks," I said to the man. The man with the orange face looked relieved, for I had seemed to warm to the room, even though it was a little boxed in. I smiled, glad to put down my rucksack somewhere safe.

"Adios, signores" and my voice was all jumped and nervous, as if someone had put a pin in my arse. The man smiled through the last gap of the closing door.

It was then I began to fret that I might not sleep at all in that room and end up going insane with insomnia for I had pictured a room with a view, and it was a dismal light. Out of the window, all I saw was a brick wall and five floors above, if I stuck my head out, I could just see the sky. The room was like a dark box, buried underground, like a basement room, and on a toilet somewhere, reverberating around the little walled back yard, I could hear someone peeing.

I lay down on the bed and hoped that I might close my eyes and try to calm down but the bed felt hard, and there was a concave hollow in the mattress for my bum and my shoulder to slot in. I observed the cream tiles on the floor. They were cold under my feet and there was also a desk, a chair and a wardrobe. The doors were double ones and they were wood panelled and the room had very clean white walls. All the windows had electric lights on, and the black-bricked wall was coated in the yoke yellow of lamp light.

Then a child started crying. I wondered if it would ever stop. I wondered if the crying was all I would ever hear again. I felt my heart begin to panic, and I could hear the little pounds it made, pounding within my chest as if it wanted to get out. I began to worry I might sit there and go mad, steadily, and then become depressed. I took off my shoes and lay back on the bed and curled up into a scared ball, looking at the window and the door as if someone dangerous might come in.

I wondered if I would be attacked by panic. Then my bladder began pestering me. It needed to relieve itself and the toilet was at the end of the corridor. It meant I had to leave my nice safe box, so I began to get myself standing again to face the outside world.

The door squeaked open in a tone of an intrigued psychoanalyst and crept out into the dark corridor, I heard muffled voices and guttural sounds - all languages, collected in the hostel rooms. I tiptoed nervously to the door, to open it and tiptoed out of my room, to the toilet. There was no-one around and I was relieved not to be seen, but I knew, as I pissed, the water tumbled noisily, and vaunted its noise to my fellow guests whose rooms faced the courtyard, and as I pee'd, I closed my eyes, glad I'd not farted.

I could hear an American woman next door, and voices rebounded around the courtyard walls, droning on, and I heard odd words:

"She just thought such a lot of herself..." "I like to be positive, but try to be realistic as well" And then sometimes the drains interrupted them, dribbling every time someone washed their armpits.

Then I leapt back to my room like a hare, doing a long jump when I got to my room, before anyone saw me. Then, once hidden away, I quickly undressed again and got under the clean white sheet.

But then, as it got darker, a thin pencil ray of sun touched my face, gently and benignly. There was a light, flooding down the courtyard, and one ray of sun poured in, straight as a ruler. I began to feel calmer and started to fantasise about Gerald's friend Adam. I pictured Adam's fluffy, cropped, dark hair. I felt his velvet black eyes looking into mine.

Dreaming about Adam made me feel lovely all over. I heard his voice in my mind, saw his lovely snub nose like a blob of butter and longed to be pretty and interesting and have things to tell him about Barcelona.

The strangest thought crossed my mind: that I might grow to like this cell perhaps even not leave it. The thought lingered, in my mind, in that lightless place, with its one ray of sun, so like returning to a womb, and my heart began to slow down, until it thumped very slowly and I felt my thoughts disappearing.

Then, with a strange calm of their own, dreams began taking the place of my thoughts, acting on a power of their own, and soon I was coated in a light sleep, like a protective skin.

I put on so many clothes as a prevention of being raped and went out to find the metro station, before getting on a train to the edge of town. I was getting pretty sick of hearing my own thoughts, and was already looking forward to human company and there was mental asylum music playing in the metro station: 'It's summertime' to the accompaniment of a drugged saxophonist and the peoples' feet clicked over the platforms robotically, making me wonder if the music was meant to make people, like opium, lethargic and directionless, so that they were easy to control, losing a sense of their real will, and going with the will of the government.

My mouth hadn't spoken for a long time now, and I wondered if I would still be able to socialise with other people at the conference. I tried to see my own reflection in the metro window, which was a rather faint impression, hoping to find an attractive sight, or, if I looked like a total idiot, and no one would want to talk to me. I saw a transparent looking face, with shy eyes and nervous bones, and decided it was far better to NOT look at my face, because it merely disappointed me, and made me lose confidence.

As soon as I looked at the conference timetable and received my badge with my name on it, I put my mind onto my work with conscientious diligence. The event was being held in a large white modern building, on the edge of town, with a glass front.

First there was a talk on Picasso and a glowing blue projector beam, aimed at the wall, informed every one of Spain's cultural heritage and Picasso's blue period.

I watched the pictures flash up on the wall, the portraits of people, each with a blue skin, and each with big sad, fat eyes and as if they wore cherry red lipstick. It seemed to me that they had drowned themselves in blue water, and looked like sad memories, lit up with moonlight. Picasso paintings looked like bits of jigsaw. Faces were broken up. The paintings are quadrilateral shapes, pieced together: doors, roofs, tossed about to look like they might metamorphose into doves and fly away, effecting the mind in a way a dream does, watery, fluid, changeable...

Everyone in the room had blue faces, and I did too, and with big interested eyes, they listened. At the end of the talk, the light flashed on. Everyone looked around at each other as if they didn't know where they were.

From the conference building I looked over at the glass window that looked over Barcelona. The rooftops were pink and orange, a clutter of terracotta, not yet seen. The cathedral bells started ringing, the outpourings of bells overlapping, each charming the ear with a different note.

As I made my way back to my hostel at the end of the day I looked about me like an animal checking for predators. I thought everyone was watching me, because my skin was so bleached, and glowed like a spot light I had dressed into my formal, conference clothes, a blue skirt, a blue blouse and brown cardigan and was sweating away. My face was wet, from sweat, and the brown cardigan was too thick for this weather.

Yet although I knew I should get safely back to my hostel room I fancied a coffee. Suddenly I saw a little cafe table in the sun and so ordered a 'cafe con leche'. The people at the tables stared ahead of them, in a dream world of their own. I felt less self-conscious to realise that and paid the waitress for my coffee.

Sitting at my table I noticed a young woman held back her head laughing while her boyfriend kissed her neck and placed his hand between her legs. The woman's legs were not covered, but bare, brown, glossy looking, with pink heeled shoes, and the man's hand was creeping up under her short skirt, stroking the thighs fondly, as if they were a separate creature attached to the woman. I was surprised. In England, no one did things like that in public, yet here it seemed a natural thing to do, as eating or walking or talking.

Another couple, at the table on my right, held one another's hands. I could see the couple's fingers, knotted gently, and placidly perched on the man's lap, and my face went all wistful, as I wondered what it would be like to be in love, imagining it was me whose hand he held. I wished I could laugh and hold back my head and have a boyfriend touch me like that.

The clothes stuck to me, for the city was so warm, and I looked drab. My clothes were drab, and I had drab bags under my eyes, and I'd been so impatient to get a tan, now my cheeks were burnt, now I thought it would be skin cancer.

Gerald had advised me to cover up my body. I looked all bundled up like a corn dolly. My brown cardigan was far too thick for this weather. And I felt invisible. No-body loved me, and every time I saw my reflection in a shop window, I saw a fool. 'How I had ever managed to feel Adam might have liked me?'

It was getting so very hot. I looked miserably at my sweaty reflection in the café window. My spots hurt, they were swollen up in the hot sun, and one of them had gone white and was full of puss. I picked at it, and saw that now; it had gone red as an apple, bursting with clear puss. Now that it stung, my eyes looked at the sight of it so sorry-looking.

When I had finished my cup of coffee at six o'clock I went back to my hotel room as planned. I was like a mummy having bandages removed, I peeled off the dark brown and blue clothes and stood and watched myself, naked. I was blotched with spots and my tits had creases in them - like trails of talcum powder under the skin. My bum sagged and I had a tampon string trailing out of my vagina, like a mouse-tail. My sweaty feet clung to the cool floor; my damp breasts were pale, breasts like plants deprived of light.

I began to wash myself at the sink, dabbing myself dry with a fresh towel and feeling the refreshing cool of moist water on my hot skin.

But then I put on a summer dress. It was short, bright coloured, decorated with yellow, orange and pink diamonds but I was too afraid of drawing attention to myself and faltered over it as I pulled it out of my case. I was pleased I'd brought it. Suddenly I longed to make myself pretty, despite the danger. I slipped on a dress barely covered the tops of my thighs. The dress was a light fabric, showing the fullness of my bare thighs and through the chest, my breasts pressed through, like cherry topped buns and my bare arms looked carefree, like fairy wings and I began brushing my hair, in the hope, that it might improve the sight of me, in the mirror. It was long hair, falling like a waterfall, thick and I stood and looked at it. I looked more colourful and prettier. Suddenly I had this longing to go back outside and explore a bit more of Barcelona in my pretty dress.

So I planned to take an evening stroll and be back at eight o'clock, when the sun began to set and as protection I pulled on my winter tights so that my legs would not show. 'By the time the rapist would have got through the gusset, to my knickers, he would be too fed up to continue, having used up all his energy getting passed my thick black tights' I thought and I pictured, in my mind, talking sensibly to the rapist, while he tugged at my tights, to get them down.

"It's not worth this, you'll go to prison for life for doing this. Why do it at all?"
However my thick black tights looked ridiculous, in such warm weather, that anyone would think I was mad. And as I considered the black tights, the two American women in the room next door were gabbling. They were talking about relationships, about liking someone enough to marry them and taking on the man's name, and I considered the issue too, for a moment, wondering how anyone could possibly like a man enough, to marry him and give up their own name for his?
As I considered this, I decided to take them off again and I took off my shoes and stripped my legs of the tights in one swift pull, and my legs were bare again. I could feel the air, gently nibbling against the skin, and it was a pleasant feeling as I picked up my bag and left my room.
"Bella" cried a lady's voice. She was looking at me smiling. I was glad and relieved to hear the cathedral bell pound, sounding like a big pan being hit by a wooden spoon, and felt carefree, showing off my bare legs and long hair, suddenly without a care.

"Have you turned the tap on Maria? This water pressure is fucking awful" Gerald asked. But I didn't answer. He was baffled, as I left him for the peace of the street. Then I thought I should have reacted, because I knew he would be suspicious again. I used to react.
The grocer wrapped up my fruit, poked his till and says, about the newspaper I was buying
"This for him?"
"He's in the shower"
"He's a lucky man" he says. I think 'Not in the shower this morning'
When I get home Gerald is pacing around.
"Did you know there were bulbs?" he says, as I'm in the door. His hair is shooting up like cropped grass, his eyes are very wild, they're squinted and he's got toothpaste on his lip.
"No" I say
"There's hundreds of bulbs in the cupboard. When did it go?" He is turning the switch on and off. I shrug.
"I dunno"
"You must remember" I clamp my teeth together, put the kettle on and focus on making my herbal tea.
"Last week sometime"
"And you've done nothing about it?"
He looks at me suspiciously as I sit quietly to eat my banana, apple. He produces a piece of paper "and we've to pay the gas bill - it's big" He takes it out as though it's evidence of a terrible crime I've committed. He stands upright over the kitchen table, with it on thrust in my face. But I stir my tea.
"Since Barcelona you don't care about anything" he said, watching me closely.

It was true. What had the Gold Man done to me? I pictured him getting out of bed and was moving calmly across the hotel room. He wandered into the bathroom, where I heard the tap water splashing. Silently I moved after him, and went to watch him.

"All right, quickly then," I said, pleased to have an excuse to stay.

Then I had felt confused, for I had expected something quick. I had expected him to want me out. But he had stepped into the bathtub, and the showerhead let strands of water shoot into the base of the bath, and he had put the plug in, so that the water was collecting in musical pools around his feet.

I stood shyly, watching his dark, baked flesh get enamelled by the spray of the shower jet, wondering what to do. He looked at me and said,

"Come" holding out a hand. Gratefully I took off my dress again, shedding myself of underwear again and I looked at him, pleased to take his large hand, stepping into the bath, while he picked up the shower and sprayed my legs. I felt his hands wash me, and the gold trailed down the inside of my thighs, like ravines that were rich, undiscovered areas of an American gold rush; I felt the hot gold rush all over me.

I held my hands in the downpour of water and scooped up water to throw against my face. I didn't speak, but when I looked at him, I saw that suddenly his face had appeared, that he had a handsome, pleasant face, with gentle eyes, still and brown and I could see the honey glow in his eyes, when he looked into my eyes and smiled, complicit.

The water chattered and hissed and gathered excitedly, pouring around our shins and he suggested we sit down, and so I found his legs around me and I was happy, seated in the soapy water that had gone a little grey and cloudy and frothy. I took his feet in my hands, and rubbed the soap against them, then rubbed his calves, and watched the milky water drip down his skin and dribble back into the bath.

Smiling, I looked at him, to check it didn't annoy him, to be washed by me, to be overbearing, but he seemed pleased, as if the act was a necessary one, he was happy about, and I looked again at his face which was tawny dark, like an ordinary man, someone I might never have noticed, with ordinary black hair and a rough shaved chin. But when he looked at me, in my eyes, my vagina hottened again, and my heart felt like melting syrup and I dropped my face while he took the soap from me to wash me, so that the touch on my skin stunned me. I couldn't move. It was a pleasant feeling, too lovely to be real, and Gerald never washed me in the bath. It was one of those happinesses I was afraid of because one worried about what hurt might accompany it. Tears that welled in my eyes at the gentleness of his touch, which was making some gaping empty hole inside me flood with warmth like an open gulf.

I let him wash me, tenderly, letting his flannel rub my chest, rub my face, my neck, and I closed my eyes, feeling the pleasure rush into my heart, as if my heart had never known such pleasure.

Then I remembered the 'ten o'clock' curfew I had told him, and did not want to seem as if I'd forgotten it. "What time is it?" I asked. He looked about him, suddenly puzzled, and stopped touching me. The steam had thickened and it seemed like we'd been in a timeless fog and then he saw my watch on the bathroom shelf, and suddenly the water was broken into fragments, like charred glass, falling around me, as he stood up and everything ceased as if I myself had broken it all.

"There is your watch," he said, as fragments fell from him as he stepped out of the bath. I remained seated, feeling gloom, as the shards of water fell over me. "It's nine o'clock," he said, wondrously. I stood up.

"I'd better go," I said, stepping out of the bath, and hoping he might offer me a towel but he was drying himself down, and didn't seem to notice my instant of hoping, before I picked up a folded one, that was on a shelf above the toilet.

I dried myself in silence, combed my hair with the comb in my handbag, and was soon back in the short dress, and stood by the door.

The Gold man came out of the bathroom. I was all ready to leave but now I could see him as he really was. He had combed his hair, while it was wet. Now it was black and shiny, with the streaks of a vinyl record. His eyelids were big, gentle blinking ones, over his deep brown eyes, and I thought how much like moths they were, when they blinked, with still a hint of gold on them, as if he wore eye shadow, so he had the look of a drag-queen, who'd just washed off his persona.

He was dressed in a beige cotton shirt, open at the chest, with loops on the shoulders, and he held something out for me and I took it and looked at it. It was the hotel visiting card.

"Here's a card for you, in case you come back. Will you come back?" I put the card in my bag, saying

"Not this summer, may be next year" and assumed he would be pleased and relieved to hear I was not hooked on him. "Are you going to go back to mime now?" The man shook his head,

"No, not now..." he replied, and paused for a moment. Then he said,

"Perhaps we could go for dinner?" I baulked.

"Dinner?" I asked. How I wanted to say yes immediately, but I worried, for, would that put him off? I faltered; afraid he would be smug to learn I was putty in his hands.

But I agreed there was time for one drink for I was feeling really reluctant to leave him. It was awful, because I was trying to seem cool, careless – and I was really relieved and disbelieving when he suggested we have dinner.

I didn't bother speaking but the gold man was asking me things, conversing with me and I felt so shy and feeble. I felt as if, for the first time, someone had woken me up inside – an inside I didn't know I had.

We went outside, the sky was navy blue and I felt him put his arm over my shoulder. It surprised me at first, feeling it over me, before smiling faintly for I rather liked it, on me, being under his arm. Usually I hated Gerald to do it and told him so, saying that it was patronising and demancipating to women, but I liked the man's arm around me, like it made my heart smile.

We walked along with the strolling tourists, whose faces were glowing in the restaurant lanterns, before he showed me to a seat.

"Let's have the aperitif here," he said. I sat quickly down, feeling greedy to be with him, and was pretending to have forgotten about my ten o'clock curfew, as if it hadn't crossed my mind but I didn't dare look at my watch, in case he saw that I knew it was nearly ten o'clock, and wondering why I wasn't leaving? Would he be worried to realise how much I liked him?

He ordered a Cinzano on the rocks and a beer for me, then told me that wine would make him sleep. Then a man walked towards us, looking all-hopeful, and distracting the gold man. He carried a bucket full of roses. Each bud was pink or yellow, white, peach or red. The Gold man spoke to him, as if he were an old friend, and then looked at me, while he held the bucket in front of me.

"Choose," he commanded. I flinched, with disbelief.

"No, no" I said, gesturing for the roses to be taken away.

"Choose," he said again, frowning. I looked back at him, as if it were a joke, unable to believe that he might be able to transform the situation into something romantic seeming, when all it was sex, and he had just picked me up in the street. He was trying to make it seem like a love film, when all it was his lust, and he was trying to disguise it by being all chivalrous, by treating me with dignity, because perhaps he felt guilty. I shrugged and purposely chose a yellow one, as if to emphasise to him that I was not participating in the idea this was romantic, by choosing a red.

He paid for it, and I noticed he paid with paper money, not the little change that he'd had in the hotel room. I worried about him wasting his precious earnings, the dribble of peseta coins, on a tourist scam, on an overpriced rose, but then I held the rose to me, pleased, and looking affectionately at the yellow yoke colour of the bud, with its satin petals and sacred interior. He looked at me and I smiled, so he gave me his look, which made my vagina start leaking again, like an old oilcan, and had that same feeling, as if a blowtorch was burning it, and then hoped he'd start chattering again, as he'd done before.

"Nothing happens for no reason" and looked at me. I looked back at him and blinked. I knew he had said something important, but was afraid to enter into the subject, preferring to let the comment float off, like some interesting but untouchable boat. "THIS hasn't happened for no reason," he said again. But I continued to be silent. If he was talking about US, it was far too out of my reach. I was juggling with the idea of me being someone he wanted a quick fuck with.

I was starting to feel sad about leaving him, when he suggested dinner. I agreed because it would mean spending a little more time with him.

"Where do you want to eat?" he asked.

"Oh just some little place that sells sandwiches" I said. I spoke rather sadly, because I knew I would have to leave very soon. I wasn't sure I'd be able to swallow anything anyway, but acted as if I was very hungry. I noticed the sky was dark now, and as we walked together though Placa Reale. There was a luke-warm air.

When we came to the other side of the square, we faltered, not knowing which direction to turn, and at this moment, we looked at one another, and embraced, spontaneously sucking one another's mouths and pulling one another's bodies towards one another. Our lips were sucked together and adrenalin shot through my heart. When I pulled away there was a red mark around my mouth and my eyes were watering.

I felt a glittering thrill run through me, looking into his dark eyes, which changed to the colour of honey. He led me into a small restaurant that was lit up with bare light bulbs, and had bare cream plaster walls, and showed me a menu, which I looked at with disappointment.

"There are no sandwiches," I said, lost. I sat, helplessly, as if now I would have to go home, for anything else was too expensive, and I didn't want to spend anymore.

"Have chicken" he shrugged. So we both dug our forks into white slices of chicken breast, surrounded by tomato salad. I was trying to fake hunger, and wanted my normal, hungry self back, with its good appetite, so that I wouldn't have to force myself to swallow. I chewed the chicken to paste, and was relieved when the waiter came to take the plate away. His eyes were still making me turn to hot coals and were changing the colour of lava, and I couldn't stop myself from looking at his eyes, all the time, until finally he stood up, throwing onto a plate, some coins and a note. I felt a pang of misery to know it was over, that I would now have to go back to my hotel.

"Well I had better go now," I said cheerfully, disguising my misery about it. I gestured the route to my hotel. "My hotel is up there," I said, feeling very sad suddenly. I thought of curling up in the tiny bed in the brick-walled room, in the disappointment of the idea of being separated from him.
"Would you like some chocolate?"
"Chocolate?" I asked
"Over there" he said, pointing to Las Ramblas. I cheered up and hoped to spend more time with him.
"I'd like some fruit" I replied. He shook his head.
"I can't get you fruit, but I can get you chocolate" I nodded at once, so he led me back down to Las Ramblas and I followed.
We came to a newspaper kiosk, still open, a beacon of light, now in the dark street. I waited, while he approached the layers of magazines. Behind the merchant, piled up like sedimentary rock cleavage, were bricks of chocolate, and something else, in a packet, which he bought as well, and slipped quickly into his pocket.
I lingered beside him, nibbling on a little chocolate. He walked me quickly back to the hotel entrance and broke off a piece of chocolate.
It was very dark now and I knew I had an early train and should really be in my room getting a good night's sleep. But then he said:
"Shall we go to my room again?" he said, with a hardly audible voice.
The Gold Man was standing on Las Ramblas waiting for my response.
As he looked at me I could feel my cervix swelling, huge as fruit, a waxen wetness seeping between my legs that I almost worried it would seep through my knickers and though my dress.

Earlier I had been standing in the same built up neighbourhood, where washing hung over balconies, kids hung out on street corners and women jabbered loudly, singing in the kitchens, clanking plates and I could smell bleach. I walked cautiously. Had I been too cocky? Would I get attacked here?

Suddenly the skin on my legs seemed almost sore with self-consciousness, without my black woollen tights. The evening air was warm, soaked in an apricot coloured light, yet I walked fearfully, looking about me uncertainly.

There was a smell of rotten vegetables and scattered on the floor, the insides of a woman's' handbag - lipstick, pearls, eye shadow and a man, routing through. It seemed to me that I was in thief land, the apartments were homes of the thieves, and, like Venice, it was not as pretty behind the scenes, behind the museums, the cathedrals, the churches, the pretty souvenir shops, behind everything with a gold veneer, there were the rundown apartments, the crumbling facades, cracked windows and the grimy alleyways and stray cats.

Then I noticed a lot of women also wearing mini-skirts pulled right up, stood on the street, looking at me pass them, with a relaxed grin. At the end of the road, the last woman, her skirt was so high; I could just see the leg of her knickers, peeking under the hem. I began to regret not having my dour, woollen clothes. My heart was pounding and I thought 'oh god, now I'm lost and the courtroom will say: you idiot, you dressed up like a tart and got lost in the red light district. You deserve every misfortune you got' and I looked about me as if I were in a trench, in world war one, about to go 'over the top'

I decided to go back and get into my black tights again and tried to make my way back to the hostel again. But then I came to the end of an alley and the sunlight had flooded it, and there was a pool of tables, round as lily leaves, with people sat at them, drinking beer, tea, coffee and glasses of green and red cordials. It was peaceful here and felt safe.

Placa St Jocep was a central square. There was a market selling pots of honey, with yellow and white striped stalls, and a group of men were playing jazz there. They had big cellos the size of rowing boats. Now I could see the form of the old cathedral, like an overgrown tree, its stone carved like beautiful sprawling bark, now that I'd worked out the layout of the town.

I was back in the tourist area and there were some stalls I knew it wasn't a howling mouth anymore - and the people weren't teeth - their psyches weren't incisors out to get a naive English woman, (in fact, if it wasn't for my spots and that wise haggard look my hair surely got my into the pretty category?)

I started to smile a little bit and noticed that people were too busy in conversations to be looking at me and I began to let myself relax. I began to stroll, looking less as though I was about to be pounced on by a serial killer, but calmer and happier. The sky was blue. I decided I would buy a sandwich and eat something on my own, and walking into a bar, I felt nervous, but acted nonchalant. Along, the bar, protected by a glass cover, were plates of omelette, liver, sausages, chorizo, paella, mussels, fish and merguez.

"Jamon" I said, with a squeak in my voice "y queso" The man's expression didn't change. His eyebrows were vivid black, his eyes wide.

"Jamon OU queso" said the man, without blinking. I chose jamon, quickly, nervously, and the man nodded, and then used a knife almost a metre long to slice away the shin of the pig's leg, which was hanging off a hook. The pig's leg had toenails like pope hats - and two big trotters, and two little trotters and skin was all stiff and yellow opaque - with the red ham blotchy underneath. "Agua el grivo" I added. He blinked a "yes", and I noticed, to my relief, that he smiled, very faintly. His neck and cheeks were plump, soft, his blue eyes kind - paternal. He had a frog in his throat, a rustling voice and his lips vibrated and spat as he spoke to someone while putting the slices of ham in a French stick for me.

Then I saw the barrow boy hurry by as if late. His barrow contained oranges, boxes of them. Seeing the delicious fruit in his barrow I realised the ham had left a salty taste in my mouth. When I bit into it, the bread broke between my teeth, and the crumbs scattered over my table. The ham was salty, rubbery and tasty and I chewed it until it turned to pulp, and all my lips were lacquered with ham grease, so that I smeared them together.

I went into the bar "Fruta? Naranja?" I asked the waiter. There were a group of women, haggling at the bar. The language sounded like catarrh in everyones' throats. Upstairs men's voices echoed, coins jingled, counters clicked and dice rattled.

The waiter shook his head

"No tengo fruta" he said.

So I left the bar went after the barrow boy, following him over the main road of Las Ramblas, where he disappeared into a large building, made of metal, with a glass roof. My thirst to eat some fruit overwhelmed me, as I tried to keep up with the barrow boy. I hurried after him and entered the building.

It was a covered market place. Inside there was a yapping of voices - a business tone that reverberated softly, a busy clacking noise, like pebbles hitting each other, like an underwater, magical place and it was a secret - hidden in a square off the boulevard. It had a cast iron ceiling of glass where the light came in the colour of vanilla ice cream and it smelt of bananas, fish, coffee, beer, citrus and the customers waved their arms, pointing at what they wanted, their eyes shifting from stall to stall, beadily, shark-like.

One bar was curtained with sausages. It had beautiful green, blue and yellow tiles decorating it. Men smiled, sleepily, as I passed, as though they remembered vaguely who I was.

I passed the olive stall, where there was every shade of green to black, shiny as marbles, sold by women with black hair, olive skins and eyes deep black looking like expresso coffee.

It was bubbling with human voices, and was warm, within, for the sun's rays heated every part of the place and there was a smell of ham.

Finally I came to the fruit stall, glowing with colour, like buried treasure. People eyed the fruits and vegetables, their prey. There were globes of fruit - magenta, yellow, lime, scarlet, cerise, all in mountains. Each vegetable was a different shape - artichokes, avocados, in rows - on a stage, like Busby Berkley performers.

I came to a stall of clementines, plums, strawberries, apples, and pears, all smelling of sweet, new fruit and looked at them as if I'd never seen fruit before. The strawberries were large as fists and shone so red. A woman in a wraparound apron began picking them up and dropping them into a bag for me.

With my stash of tempting fruit I made off to find a park bench on which to sit and eat it.

I walked up the boulevard under the trees but there was no sight of a bench and I got distracted by a pet stall and the jabbling and squeaking of little chicks and light green parrots, flinging themselves around their cages. Inside some boxes with bars on the front were more parrots, green and shrieking. White doves were for sale, with blackcurrant blinking eyes, hamsters rolled up like cotton wool, hens, cheeping, horrified ducklings with mink feathers, yellow as omelette; and there were tropical fish, like fireworks, orange, sapphire blue, emerald; and terrapins.

Then I stopped at a flower stall, full of rows and rows of colours, clashing with one another, yoke, tomato red, sunset lilac - all stashed in buckets, as if screaming out to be noticed, frilled, dazzling, shaded by the trees above. There were chrysanthemums and roses, pink, red, salmon, tangerine... fat women and quiet sweeping men guarding them, while children with wet eyes and shiny noses wandered passed with reaching fingers and poodles with wide black eyes and cone noses whimpered at the foot of chairs.

And finally I stopped at a gold statue.
When he had stared at me with that stony look, I had felt uneasy and moved away from him. I had felt afraid.
I had gone to sit down on the grass of the Placa Catalunya, to eat my strawberries. The strawberries had now melted and gone slushy in the hot plastic bag and they dripped like pieces of stewed meat, staining my butcher hands. I dropped them onto my tongue, munching, and chewing, until red liquid seeped from the corners of my mouth, not bothering to wipe up the juice. I licked my fingers, which were sweet, delicious, the strawberry pulp torn by my teeth; the seeds crunching like shards of glass.
The strawberries reminded me of men's noses and chins, the seeds like deep pores and bristles, pointed and shiny red as blood. The sun was hot, stuck like glue to my face and my belly was full of fruit: a whole punnet of giant strawberries (my fingers sticky with cochineal)
Lovers wandered passed, birds, pigeons created a wind - flapping their wings like blankets over me. The only moving creatures around my face were the male pigeons, which puffed up their feathers and turned themselves into lions with bushy manes, flicking around the floor like a black and white movie.
It was like a beach, the grassy hill covered in people who were sitting and lying around in the sun, lazy and motionless. A group of men blew into wooden flutes, Mexican men, wearing blankets and sombrero hats. The sound was a soft, windy melody, which rippled through the square.

I lay down on the grass, letting my hair tumble in the fag ends and bits of sweet wrappers that lay in the grass. I felt a breeze, heard a voice, felt laughter. I noticed the man's brown eyes everywhere, in men and women, looking about everywhere, with eyes like the Gold Man's had been. The open air was their theatre, the audience, the people in the street, and I peered, in astonishment, as two people, right next to me, nuzzled and purred like cats, on a park bench, their eyes dilating and smiling, shaped like sunflower seeds.

Gerald never looked at me like that, nor I at him. These couples: their bodies were twisted around each other like the ribbons of a Maypole. The men were putting their hands on bare thighs, letting them stroke the area under the skirt, while the women allowed them to, careless of anyone seeing it happen, as if they couldn't believe their eyes to see the trick inside their eyes.

I closed my eyes and a strange thing happened. My mind paint images of naked people and though afraid, of what this might do, what dangers it might draw to me; I couldn't help having sexual fantasies. I pictured, while on the grass, the sight of a naked woman, with dark hair, quiet eyes, a woman I'd seen in a film, who had passionately stripped off the clothes of a man, another actor, and, scrambling to the floor, they had fucked one another, as if famished, as if they'd just endured a lifetime absent of love, and, for that short secret moment, behind the backs of their husbands, their wives, on a kitchen floor, they were having a moment of pure loving passion, before returning to the domesticity of daily married life, never having said a word to each other.

Suddenly I hankered for a lover, hankered to be mauled and kissed by someone and I debated, vaguely, whether it would be worth being unfaithful, if this would teach me if I had true love with Gerald?

The strawberries were furry, fruity and full of strawberry juice and my belly was soon a mush of fruit, and it bulged. I felt it churning as I walked, like a soft Kenwood mixer Soon my hands were cochineal, and I licked on them, as though trying to disguise evidence of a bloody crime.
I felt the sun stare straight at my face, like a fierce acidic spray valve, stinging my eyes, and it was beginning to feel like a cat's claws, clawing my skin.
The city was bathed in sunlight and warm air and there was a hissing sound, like a whisper of excitement.
I came across the park, so I went inside. There was a fountain, which fizzed with water. There was a monument, with a Roman chariot and four horses; an arch with cherubs sitting on it, holding up bunches of grapes; a naked woman lying on her side, and dancing women, standing on big shells, with men with beards, ogling at them. I listened to the sorbet white water, pouring down the stone stairway, where four dragons paced, water shooting out of their nostrils, wings like spider webs, before lifting up my face, to smell the air. There was pungent scent of wild lilies.
I could feel the ends of my brown hair tickle my arse and I was regaled by more wolf whistles and I did not care that I was awakening men's interest.
My shoulders felt all calm, like soft cushions and I could smell the grass, newly cut, and hear the laughter and chatter of people. I wandered towards the spread of lawn, where pigeons with splayed wings like feathered fingers, and rose up into the faraway sky like rhododendron petals blowing away. The people were sitting, lying, wandering, enjoying the sun's limelight, and only the old women shuffled in the mottles made by the leaf shadows.

I roamed my way through the park, looking about me, at a park soaked with sunlight, so that the palm trees glistened like Christmas tinsel. The park smelt of the bitter scent of deep green fir trees, and it sounded to me as if sugar fell, between the tree cracks, from a sky that was a perfectly dyed and unblemished azure blue, which had only faded to a pale white just around the sun, which blazed like a bleach spot.

I wondered if I had found heaven, particularly because there were no wasps, no bees, just wispy flies that were getting swayed by the breeze (if anything spoilt summer, I thought it was the wasps) and it seemed that the sun was a glorious and a ginormous shower, giving a plentiful amount of heat to everyone.

I even wondered if I saw, before me, a miracle, after the long, bone bare winter, for, spring was back, and from nothing, suddenly, the park was an abundance of bushes and greenery.

I could not leave it. Children were bleating like lambs, beneath the trees, that seemed to each be a different shape: oval, towering tall, or looking like a minarets or a fountain or the plume of feathers on a cockerel, each coloured a different green: viridian, ochre, forest green. Birds chirped everywhere, singing like squeaky toys, hidden by green leaves stretching like pee-green hands, to protect them. Then two terriers quickly ran toward one another, seeking one another's genitals, sniffing one another, bristling and spasming. Young couples, holding one another's hands, and unself-consciously, they would put their mouths together, licking the inside of their mouths, then, continue walking, looking satisfied.

My breasts pushed through the pink and yellow dress, and I found it was titillating to get male glances, and I wanted to be noticed, for I needed to be noticed so badly, in case I dissolved to nothing, like someone who'd never existed.

But then I gathered my things and sat up from my reclined position and my eyes fell on a citadel on the top of a hill. It reminded me of a fairy tale palace. It stood, like on a page of a child's picture book, almost faded by vapour, looking down from above Barcelona,

Inspired by the sight of it, I started walking towards it. All of a sudden my map was my own heart, and I found that my feet were walking me to the park exit. I cut through the little roadways, in the quieter part of town, where washing hung from balconies, scooters sounded like giant wasps and women watched me from doorways, their children on plastic wheelie toys.

At the foot of the hill, I bought a ticket for the funicular, from a small hut and sat in the little car that moaned its way wearily up the hill, whimpering like a tired puppy. At the top, I walked out, to find the sandy walls of the castle, turreted, ruined. Over the edge of the cliff top, I could see a vast sea. It looked like a vast spread of diamonds, infinitely twinkling, and I gazed in wonder, then at the sight of Barcelona, a valley, filled with yellow and pink blocks of buildings, jig sawed together like a cubist collage.

Then I watched how the sun melted into the blue horizon, like a melting scoop of peach melba ice-cream, coating everyone with its orange, so that everyone changed colour, and the soft warmth made me sit on the wall, the light stroking me gently.

I longingly watched the many couples passing me by. They held hands, drifting with the calm breeze, smiling at one another. I was eyeing their linked hands like someone shunned, forgotten, and alone, sat on the wall and I wished someone might hold my hand like that, take me out for dinner, wine me and dine me, and I dreamed of a lover, but stood up, finally, with a breath of resignation, preparing myself for another evening alone, eating a ham bocadillo.

I had joined the crowd, treading lazily down Barcelona Citadel's steps, as the cooler evening air began to trickle in, making their way home and it had been a quick walk, back to the centre of Barcelona, and now the cafes were full of people. It must have been nearly eight. The light bulbs were hanging on strings, attached to the tree tops, looking like pearl necklaces, all brightly lit, while, at the tables, people made the noise of murmuring seals, laughing and talking, while I treaded a little sadly to find a cheaper cafe in a less touristy area, with only enough money left to buy a ham bocadillo.

But then I saw a crowd had gathered on Las Ramblas. Peering over someone's shoulders, and I saw the gold statue again and I wondered once again about the stony look he had given me the day before, the serious look, and I was still curious, still curious to know why he had looked at me like that?

6

Then Gerald caught me going downstairs to look at the mail.
"Why do you keep getting the mail? You've never been expecting anything before?"
"I'm just waiting for my bank statement"
That really got him suspicious.
"Why would you want to look at that?" He screwed up his eyes.
"I don't know" I said. I didn't know why I was feeling hurt. The Gold Man had just wanted sex, hadn't he?
I had entered the Gold Man's hotel lobby a second time, no-one asked me for my passport and he opened the door of his hotel room to see the unmade bed, the sheets washed like sea ripples, frozen in time since our last stormy love making.
Each of us undressed ourselves, more confident, more certain, more quickly this time. This time he took off his clothes and stood with his penis, all enormous again. He was quiet, stretching the rubber over it, and then he knelt right up to my bottom hole and shoved his penis right in!
"Ow" I cried, in shock.
"You will like it," he said; with a new snarl in his voice. I looked hurt, to hear the snarl, as if a big bad wolf had emerged, from his old self and while I endured it, and was prodded again, I was getting confused. I was trying not to, but I was rigid with fear.
"But it hurts," I argued, appalled. He reached over to his bedside table, and picked up a bottle of sun cream.
"Put this on" he said "to make it wet... to lubricate" I'd read that sun cream destroyed condoms and that it was dangerous and risky for catching Aids and so I pulled away from him.
"No" I squealed. And this time I stood up.

Suddenly I was alarmed and disappointed. He had changed. I looked at him appalled, for from being so romantic, now he didn't seem to care.
"You'll enjoy it, you'll enjoy it," he said, as if I was being tiresome.
"No" I said, with a second squeal, hurrying to the bathroom and locking the door. Wretchedly I stood in the bathroom with the door locked. My heart was beating. He had become a wolf! He only wanted sex! All that romance, was just tricking me. He had enticed me there, just to trick me and hurt me! .
I sat on the toilet seat and watched the floor dimly. It must have been very late now, after midnight, but I had no idea of the time and yet I didn't want to leave him.
I still wanted him, but felt afraid to go out to him again, trying to breath and calm down. I was bolted in and I wondered what on earth I was going to do to get out?
I stood in the bathroom a while, in the white, bright light. It was pristine clean. I felt, how scared, how weak, how I was not a tough woman at all, but someone hurt, with feelings.
I felt tears come to my eyes, and I felt frightened to feel so vulnerable. It felt as if everything calm and sensible had been wrecked. He had seemed greedy and heartless and changed.
Then I washed my face, cleaned myself, stroking cool water between my legs (which was like a hot morsel of meat). Then I just knew I had forgotten time and place. The longer I sat there, the more I calmed down.
After a while, I wondered how he was. What was he doing? Had he left the room? What was he really thinking? I began to wish I could have pleased him, that he'd not seen my terror, my weakness and vulnerability. Now he had seen how vulnerable I was, and how unhappy I was, that all I was to him was a person he wanted to fuck.

But I began to want to know how he was. I undid the bathroom lock and went back into the bedroom. He was lying on the bed, his eyes closed, but then he opened them and looked at me, only now his eyes seemed less interested in me. They were disappointed and quiet, and he seemed to be sulking a little.

I lay down beside him and smiled, hoping my smile might make everything better, that he might forget my scared, cowardly side.

Hoping to please him, I took the penis carefully in my hand, and squeezed it a little between my fingers, enjoying, suddenly, how it stiffened gradually and grew in size. It was no longer floppy, but rigid and thicker and a dome had formed at the end of it, which had a speck size hole with a drop of dew coming out of it. I smiled as if something naughty about me had been successful and he looked at my face with his simple brown-eyed look. He rolled over and kissed me again and touched my sore vagina,

"In the big hole" I said and heard, with alarm, how my voice sounded like a little girls. He put his penis in again but very quickly he pulled it out and lay on his back, as if tired.

"I can't do anymore," he said. His attitude seemed changed. He was vague and distant and I wondered if he had lay on his back, not because he was fifty and tired, but because he had gone off me totally. I also wondered if I had a floppy cervix and he couldn't create friction and that was why he had tried the bottom hole.

The clock read two in the morning and I stared at the minutes clicking by and listening to him breath. The lamp was still switched on, but he had closed his eyes, and was beginning to snooze in a lovely peace.

I knew I shouldn't have overstayed my welcome. I knew I should leave. The novelty had worn off. Now he let his penis flop on his belly, so that it slapped on the tummy, a lazy, tired flap, and he closed his eyes and snoozed, and I assumed he must have 'gone off' me. I hoped he might change his mind, and lay hopefully beside him, wanting our bodies to touch. I waited anyway, and lay beside him, putting my head on his heart, to hear the gentle drumming. It sounded like the drumming of fingers, and I lay listening to the sound.

I assumed that the moment I was in love, they knew it. They sensed it, and they were bored, instantly bored, as if there was no more challenge and the seduction process was over. Like an empty balloon he continued to drowse in the big white bed. I had risen to the state they had wished for. Now there was nothing else to do and the game was over. I sensed it. I lifted my hand and touched his doughish penis, smiling, but the penis had shrunk, and so I put it down, as if I didn't care.

So because he was sleeping and snoring lightly, and because of the calmness of his heart while my own heart beat so loudly, and not only loudly, but noisily, so that I could hear it myself, pounding, almost as noisily as a clock ticking, showing my real feelings, showing how I'd been affected by this brief encounter I decided I should get away.

I was not sleeping. I was anxious and afraid, and left on my own. Perhaps he was being colder on purpose so I would get the picture that it was over - his passion for me was exhausted? Stabs of hurt hit me; hurt I hadn't felt for years, ricocheted into me. I didn't want him to see me, see that I was hurt, that I was nervous and afraid now. My body was getting all taut, my bones were like coat hangers and my stomach, tight, like tightened violin strings.

I could feel that I had fallen in love, I knew it and it felt just like the other times, straight away, and as soon as affection came for men, they would take away their interest, leaving me to have them on a pedestal, while I myself had sunk down to being nobody. I didn't want him to see my all low in esteem. I wanted to get away, get away fast, hide all my wounds, my mess, and my nervousness.

So I got out of bed to dress and prepared myself to leave. A path appeared in my mind, the path to my hostel. I wanted to go alone, I liked my pure image at the hostel and I liked my single, crisply sheeted bed.

His eyes stayed closed while I dressed and he breathed softly. His peaceful indifference, I envied it, wishing I could sleep so peacefully, and as I dressed, my clothes felt like bandages, winding around me to cover up my wounds, my beating heart. He continued to sleep and just as I got to the door I stopped, looked at him. I loitered in the doorway and eyed him for last time, perhaps to see any last sign of affection. I just didn't want to leave, but it seemed to me that, besides a quick shag, what other use was I to him? Wanting to get away from him as quickly as possible, I opened the door and just as I opened the door, all at once, he opened his eyes and looked at me.

"Stay," he said "I'll get you an early morning call if you want," I felt happy, for an instant, hearing him suggest that… wanting me to stay. But then I noticed his sleepy eyes and felt envious to see his red eyes, and jealous of how sleepy he looked. I thought about how uncomfortable it would be, lying beside him, for the whole night, listening to him peacefully sleeping when I felt so wired and miserable and mixed up, and how dull his voice, how little it seemed to want me to stay now and I couldn't be with someone who didn't feel the same way for me.

I wanted the black, cool street - to go out - leaving him behind, the yellow lamp shining on his bronzed skin, leaving that feeling of love behind forever. I went to the door to put my hand on the door handle, as if needing its support. He shrugged and got out of bed, throwing on some clothes.

"I'll walk you back," he said. I felt encouraged again hoping he might stay with me now. My heart lifted, but I acted as if it wasn't important,

"Oh no, it's all right, stay and sleep" I replied.

"It's dangerous," he insisted.

He got out of bed and I wondered if he cared enough to come and see my small hostel room? He began to thread his legs into the leg holes of his boxer shorts. He dressed sleepily and then pulled up his black trousers. Once again he was buttoning up the beige shirt, leaving the top three buttons undone so I could see the thick swirl of his black chest hair, while I stood by the door, watching him dress. Then he seemed to be searching for something - through his laundry and his bags.

"What are you looking for?" I asked.

"I'm looking for a present to give you," he said, perking up a little. I cheered up. Did he still care for me?

"I've got a present - I've got the rose'" I answered, in 'don't feel guilty, you've already been charming enough' tone, so he shrugged and we left the room in silence, walking side by side, up the street.

A woman passed us in the street and smirked at him. When he smiled at her, I felt worried. Maybe I too was just a vehicle for him to get sexual pleasure? I was trying to relax. The moon was aglow like the street lamps and the buildings were a grave dark grey, the shutters of the windows closed up. Except for the purple and gold lights of the casino, everything else was in darkness. Down an alley, I could see a woman on her knees. A man stood, his groin in her face – her mouth was on his penis. She moved her head, her mouth over the penis – it was so fast – like a woodpecker, pecking I tried to keep myself cheerful but I wondered what I had just done, who he was, this stranger with his arm around me?

Now his hand dangled over my shoulder like a wet cloth, as if I maybe he'd put it there out of faint courtesy. I could hardly speak from the shrapnel of emotions. A woman passed us by. Her mascara was smeared down her face, as if splats of mud. There were wet marks around her eyes, and her eyes were bloated and dismal. A stern faced man walked along beside her, like he was a soldier, leading her to a prison camp.

"People get very sad at this time of night" Juan Carlos said simply.

We slowed down at Placa Jaumes. It was dark and desolate now.

"You can leave me here if you want" I said, hoping to be unseen by him. My voice was high pitched, strange to me and I was struggling to keep myself together, letting my fingers dangle in his belt, and my buttocks felt strange and suddenly I farted, and heard my tight voice cry out "excuse me", before blushing and worrying that my breath stunk from worrying, for the gasses slipped out of the slackened buttocks he'd just buggered and made this loud, squirty noise. "It's alright. I'll walk you right back to your hostel." He shrugged. I felt encouraged.

"You should come to Covent Garden in London. There's mime there. Business would be good," I said, but he just nodded disinterestedly so I felt stupid saying it.

I looked at his arm, relaxed, hanging down by his side, no longer around my shoulder. Then we arrived at the door of my hotel; the huge door loomed above us, far too big for people, made for giants. All the windows of the hostel were in darkness.

"Thank you for a lovely evening" I said, feigning cheer. He stood there, smiling back at me, his soft gentle eyes, gentle to the last. I put my hand on the black hairs of his chest, just to show some affection. He smiled, raised his hand to wave at me. "Good luck" he said. It was the last thing he said, before he went. Nothing in his eyes wanted to hold on to me, I was sure of that. And that was why he let me go so easily, not even asking for my address.

Then he took his warm, sparkling brown eyes, somewhere else, out of my reach, and I turned from him quickly to ring the entry bell.

The doors clicked open and I ran into the hotel with my hurt to throw it into the darkness of the stairs. I slipped by the desk, where somewhere in the room behind, a television screen gave off a blue light but I closed my door after me, stripping off my clothes in the darkness.

"You're brown," Gerald had said. I was glowing and usually I was pale, so he frowned. "Did you have a good time?" He watched me with suspicious, steely eyes and smelt strange to me. It felt like I was hugging a stranger and I was wishing the hug would affect me, as if hugging him for a longer time - like a battery charger - might increase the energy, the energy of love. I wondered where it had gone.

He had recently cropped off all his hair, cutting off the colour and softness so it looked like iron filings. Through his glasses his red eyelids seemed to have shrunk, so I hurried to the kitchen to put the kettle on, not wanting Gerald to look at me closely, in case he noticed the change in me.

Gerald followed me, already interested in the fact that I hadn't continued hugging him for very long.

"Aren't you going to hug me again?" he asked. He went nearer and put his arms around me but I stiffened. "You haven't seen me all this time" I let him put his hands around me but when I smelt him, I felt a repulse. "Hey!" he said, in surprise, as I pulled away.

When I arrived in London, Gerald's and my flat seemed like an unknown place, brightly lit with spring light but the furniture and walls were sparse, like a desert. All that covered the floor were golden quadrilaterals, made by the light, coming in whenever it pleased. Outside the window was a bushy tree, being shaken as if a cheerleader girl had got a hold of it, sounding like a rustling dance tutu.

I put down my bag.

"Gerald?" I called but there was no answer, so I took my bag to the bedroom and began to take out my dirty clothes. I listened to the news on the radio and wished, all at once, that I hadn't, for I heard the headlines: a man in Cyprus purposefully gave his girlfriend Aids. I stopped, and turned pale, hearing how the man had known he had the disease, and had knowingly infected his beloved. At once, my heart began to beat very fast, and I felt weak at the knees, for the idea came to my mind that perhaps Juan Carlos had had the very same thing in mind. Perhaps he was in fact a bitter man who wished to infect me? In my mind, Juan Carlos transformed from being a saint to being a murderer secretly wishing to murder me. Perhaps that was why he wanted to use the sun cream, knowing it would destroy the condom?

But then I pictured the condom, safely on, and went to get an atlas, to see where Argentina was, hoping it was miles from Brooklyn, or any other Aids infested place. I remembered that he never told me where he was from in Argentina, and maybe that was because he didn't want me to track him down. I sat there, for a while, nervously, until before long, I could hear footsteps coming up the stairs, and when the door opened.

I ran into Gerald's arms, clutching at him like a limpet against his rock hard chest.

"This is new," he said, surprised "Why so clingy?" He watched me, suspiciously, but I ignored him, hugging him, hoping that my fear might go away now that I was in his arms.

"I love you," I said, while hugging him.

On the train back to Paris I had closed my eyes. But as soon as I closed them, I began thinking about the Gold Man's body, reconstructing it in my mind, like jigsaw pieces. There was his chin - with the little crease and rough as sandpaper, and his lips, thin lips, (but he flapped his tongue like a fish out of water) and his nose and his magician's eyes that took control of me and when I looked to my right, I jolted to find someone sitting beside me on the train and I hoped it was him.

Then, when I opened my eyes, I saw the same tawny hands, with plump fingers, the same plump fingers as Juan Carlos sitting next to me on the train. They were golden brown, the large hands that had touched my breasts, and as soon as I saw them I recognized them. They were his hands! I felt an incredible joy rush through me: extraordinarily beautiful, big, soft and tawny and with a great jolt, like electricity, of excited happiness, I thought 'He's followed me and found me!'

Only, when I turned to look at the face with a big smile, my smile went away. I saw instead a different man. His face was grey and he had a hooknose, with dull, empty eyes, empty of life and emotion. It was not Juan Carlos. I turned my face away, to look out of the window. I felt an ominous disappointment soar through me.

I had thought that time would wear him away, but as the train was skidding back north, like it was a toboggan, skating over a sheet of ice backwards I was feeling bleak. I passed chateaux, churches, villages and though farms surrounded by ballooning hills of yellow rape, away from the southern heat, trying to imagine Adam's face, but I could only smell Juan Carlos in my hair, on my hand, and it aroused me.

I was sure that he would begin to go from my mind. But waking up the next morning in my Paris hotel room I pressed yesterday's dress to my nose, just to breath in the scent of him. He was still on it! I searched through my clothes for any trace of his smell, any of his hairs. I fell on my knees, to go through my bag, tenderly putting my clothes to my nose. Pressing the garments to my face for any trace of his scent.

I found one of his hairs, short, pitch black. It must have been his pubic hair. I wanted to keep it, yet didn't know where to put it. It was a tiny, coiled black hair, coal black and thick, and I sat in the dim room, inspecting the hair, as if it was the last part of someone who had died. I did not know why, but I couldn't throw it away, and ended up putting it in between the yellow petals of the rose, planning on pressing it, and then I didn't want to shower the smell of the gold man off me and I filled with this tremendous sorrow that I would have to, and never be able to smell him again.

I was sure he'd done magic on me, for all of a sudden I wanted him again. I needed to shower and pack, but all I could do was just lie still with my eyes closed, seeing my time in Barcelona, where I'd had no one to please, no-one to think about, just getting on with my daily plans, and not being afraid. When the hands had belonged to someone else, someone with dull eyes and my heart felt depressed. I couldn't throw away his rose, or the pubic hair and I kept standing up for myself for having been unfaithful, arguing with myself, as if it was the right thing to do and I wasn't just manipulated by a master seducer.

As the day went on I tried to get back to the person I was. I pictured being with Gerald again. I pictured our life together. I pictured his security.

But on looking in the mirror, I wondered if there was a change in me: on the outside? I wondered if I looked any different, from the cowardly scarecrow I usually was and stared at myself in the reflection. Though I saw my reddish face, and thought it looked a bit sore, I looked healthier and my hair was fairer, bleached by the hot Spanish sun. I was sure I looked pretty and freer, even less shy, less unsure of myself. My eyes were relaxed and lips softer and I smiled quicker - the nerves less manacled and my stomach wasn't tight anymore.

Tears for Fears, the pop group sang "Shout, shout, let it all out... you shouldn't have to sell your own soul" and I thought how often I sold my soul to Gerald. It was called compromise, but part of me was not really happy compromising, and parts of me didn't want to go home, not after knowing my soul's desire for I had had a treasure of a time.

I felt different, as if I was not the same person I had been on the outward journey. I felt I could be friendly with strangers, if I liked them, and as if I didn't belong to anyone (for so long I had assumed I belonged to Gerald) Then I tried reading a book to distract me, but every time I tried to focus on my book, I kept wanting to get back to what was exciting me most: my memory of Juan Carlos, and I sat, heaving and yearning for him and his red, luscious cock.

From the little round window of the ship, going back across the English channel, I saw how the sun was like shredded satin ribbons, blowing and fluttering over the sea's surface and out of the boat's window the crests and waves that flopped forward, then up, then forward again, reminded me of Juan Carlos, the way he had made love, and before long, I was thinking about him again, how he had been so athletic, and moved so much, because of a lifetime of tennis, and he must have been forty or so, but he seemed so young and I wondered what he'd seen in me, me, with my sunburnt pink face and the orange and yellow dress.

I should have been happy to be going home. I should have been relieved to be going back to my secure flat in Islington, safe with Gerald. But Britain, with its ousts, looked so faded. A tired evening sunlight, just strong enough to spill over the grey roofs, could be seen as the coach drove in to London, and Blackheath had appeared again, all glittering green, and as the coach crossed over it, it seemed to hover over a peaceful green lake, bathed in gold sun, and I imagined the sun soaking into the ground, to warm the skeletons buried there after the black death, but when the coach passed though Deptford, the bars seemed too dusty and the boys, with their hands in their pockets and trainers too big for them, seemed bored by the road ahead.

It began to feel like I was going home to a prison where there were so many standards expected of me.

I got off the bus to find Essex Road empty. The pavement was blazed with sunlight and there was a smell of greenery. Now my expected fate was to be with Gerald, and though relieved to be going back to the wedding plans, strangely I felt a great weight and I didn't understand why. I was glad to have Gerald, to have my stable life, yet I was sorrowful that it was over with the gold man. It had been so short, too sweet, and now it had gone and I couldn't catch its butterfly memory.

I prepared to hug Gerald and slot back into my old life. He would put on the TV and we would eat from a plate in front of it as we did every night.

I took the yellow rose out of my bag and dropped it in the bin. It had been bent by the journey, the stalk was folded in two - and now it was a little crushed. This rose, perfumed, was the only thing I had of him, as well as the little card with his hotel address on it.

I knew now that I must have no evidence of my Gold Man. He must be forgotten.

However, moments later I went back to the bin. I furrowed my way through the rubbish and pulled out a yellow rose again. I pushed it to the back of the drawer and closed the secret drawer, carefully,

8

Gerald began kissing my limp lips. He undid his zip and pointed to his flaccid penis, making a hurt puppy dog noise. It took just a flick of a thought to get Gerald's penis electric stiff and sex was done that much it had become like a chore every time he was aroused.

I unzipped his office trousers and got down on my knees. I took his penis in my hands. But while it stiffened like a rolling pin, I felt bored. I thought it looked like a spring roll, waiting to be fried and then I got pubic hair caught in my mouth and yawned. It was like moulding plastercine and salty water sprung up in the crater at the end and while he was fixated on having it licked and I wished for some coca-cola as it tasted of stale oats.

"I love you," I said to Gerald. I thought it would be easy to keep it a secret but as I kissed him and we closed our eyes and moved towards the bed, it seemed like a long, dull time having sex, where I was uninspired, going through the usual positions, and though I pretended to like it, there was no 'pepper' and no 'spice'.

"Aren't you excited about the wedding?" Gerald asked, glancing at me sharply.

He didn't smile, it seemed that his eyes were cold and green, and what seemed strange was that when I looked in them, they caused me to feel nothing at all.

We were sitting in the living room, watching television. The window was open. The sky was blue and pigeons scattered into the sky like fireworks. Primrose light fell from the sun like snow and outside the gardens were a party of dandelions.

"What happened in Barcelona?" he asked

"It was an excellent conference," I said. We watched the scribble of images on the television; I felt his fingers sweep over my neck like a wave. He stroked my neck as if I was a domestic cat. I turned to look at his face. A dominant white hair was coiling between his ginger hairs. I noticed how there was a frizzled quality to the end of his eyelashes and wondered if he'd burnt them with a match. "I didn't enjoy myself, I was lonely," I told him. His skin was like sour milk and I forced a smile and my stomach tightened.

For the next few days I tried to return to the old life. I tried to act as if nothing was wrong with me.

But I couldn't help going to sit on the bed, thinking that the furniture looked so lonely, so cold. I looked up at the light bulb, and felt it burn into my eyes. The buildings across the way were turning black, and their lights were being switched on, so that the windows looked like rectangular jewels embossed in lead and the orange streetlights sent an oxidising sheen over them.

Like a black hole, or an abyss, I considered the emptiness of life without my Gold Man. He was now a ghost, and he lingered like a perfect person in the back of my mind and I hadn't felt excited since my evening with Juan Carlos (except moments thinking about him) and it came to me that maybe he had put something in my drink to make me want to go back to him: an addictive drug? Perhaps that was why I was shaking earlier: withdrawal? Cold Turkey? Maybe, with him, my brain let off so many happy, loving cells I became addicted to them and longed for them again? That evening had been equivalent to three ecstasies.

I realised, with regret and with sadness, that my brain had become befuddled and unrealistic, and that I was being really very ungrateful, for here I was facing a man that genuinely loved me, had spent nine years with me (and not just the one night) and was offering me marriage. I was being truly ungrateful, and outrageously unrealistic, because all the time I was thinking about some mime artist, and marrying him instead! Should Juan Carlos have offered me marriage, I would have dropped everything, and I even felt that I would have his children, give up everything, as though he had total power over me. I wondered if he'd sensed that I was ready to surrender to his every wish, and that 'put him off'? Some men liked the challenge of a conquest with a woman. They like to work at winning her, they like there to be friction in their striving for power, and with me, Juan Carlos had sensed that I was ready, that night, to be taken to an altar and filled with every baby he wished for.

I looked out at the tree outside, fluttering all over like a hive of bees, and suddenly felt as if I was looking with stale eyes, as if I'd seen it before. I knew human beings should move on, and, like the Native Americans, travel and camp in different places, and not get stale and stuck in one place. Life was a journey, an ever-changing journey, with new facets to it, and yet I looked at Gerald and felt in a rut, not on a path, not on an adventurous path at all. Then one night while Gerald slept I couldn't sleep. I lay away tossing and turning. I longed for the gold man, as if I had been struck with fever. Already the birds were ringing like bells and the sky was starting to go navy blue and pale. Gerald's breath hissed, and I lay, longing for Juan Carlos. I had a sprinkle of sweat on my face, as if I had a fever, and my face looked pained from wanting him. I closed my eyes, hoping to sleep again, but I ached, and yearned and longed, and opened them as if the effort of closing them, of keeping them closed, had been too difficult.

I looked up at the ceiling hopelessly, and pictured Juan Carlos, so at peace, in his ignorant state of picking up women in the street, cosily flattered by their interest in him, before letting them leave his room after he had fucked them. I'd been his victim, ensnared by him, seduced, and then, at the end, I'd seen the dead look in his eyes. I had been dead to him. At the end of the night, I was no longer alive to him. He'd seduced me and now there was no point, he'd already strangled me to death. Gerald was sleeping and silently I undressed. I put my fingers and my knuckles all into a ball and hoped I could do what Aborigines do - reach Juan Carlos psychically and make him come and find me.

My face was greyer then it had been and my eyes were slunk and stewed. I sat up and looked about me. Every time I closed my eyes, I thought of his brown eyes. I felt trapped, as if I were in prison. I wanted to cry.

I got out of my bed and tiptoed over to the door. The leafy trees outside hissed and murmured, heaving and thick. The street was dark and empty. When I reached the top of the stairs, there was a sound of steam seeping from a slow cooker, but it was Gerald, his bulbous form wrapped up in the duvet in the darkness.

I kept as still as I could, but felt as if I might burst and walked in a circle in the darkness, looking out at he dark street. Then I sat on the settee, unable to rest calm, I had to take out the yellow rose. Gerald never looked in the drawer, for, not only was it hard to open but when it did, it made a shrieking noise because the wood needed planing down and it was full of only my bits and pieces.

The rose's mystery remained hidden in the drawer, but tucked inside its cellophane wrapper was a black pubic hair. I held the pubic hair between my fingers and looked at it. My face was pained and sad. Also hidden in the wrapping was an address. It was the address of the hotel of the Gold Man and I took it to the table. I looked at the address for a long time. I lay down on the sofa, to close my eyes and let my mind dwell on him. I imagined his lonely brown eyes, in that hotel bed, haunted by the memory of me and I pitied him, and felt worried all of a sudden, wondering whether he was thinking about me all the time too?

I went to the kitchen to make a cup of tea. The fridge seemed to pant like a hot dog, and buzzed continuously like an electric razor. Occasionally, a car outside sounded like someone was vibrating their lips. I looked out of the kitchen window, while waiting for the kettle to boil. My eyes were big and sad, and somehow I felt trapped, and yet I didn't know why.

It was a bit cooler, and air poured into the kitchen. It was a slightly mild night that smelt of green leaves and pollen. A dog in a downstairs' yard was squealing like a rusty tricycle, its chain jangling as it rushed about its yard. "Why was he going around and around in my head?" It was no use thinking about him, because he had just wanted to see if he could snare me into sex and perhaps he was a genius of seduction, standing on the pedestal, for that only purpose. His eyes were like the holes of guns, and he must have seen me, in the pink and yellow dress, flirting, all feathery and wild, and his eyes took aim on me. Rather than doing his job, he was eying up 'talent' in the street. But my stomach continued to be tight and I was so awake and wired, it felt like I'd had a year's supply of coffee and so I took a glass and filled it with water, and tried to concentrate on drinking the water in big gulps, trying not to think about Juan Carlos, but each time I tried, I imagined his brown eyes looking at me and when they did, I felt warm, lovely, excited.

Then I crept back to the living room and decided to write him an angry letter. I slowly eased open the drawer, and took out a pen. It squeaked on closing, and I glanced around at Gerald anxiously, but he was sleeping deeply. I sat with a piece of paper in front of me, chewing on the end of my pen. I wanted to tell him he was the first man who couldn't make me come, that he was an awful mime artist, short, stodgy and thin haired AND that he was just a tennis veteran.

'Dear Juan Carlos,

If you think you've got me to fall in love with you, you are very much mistaken. I fuck men I hardly know all the time, blue men, white men and any colour men. There's nothing special about YOU, and I am very much in love with my boyfriend,

Yours,' and I signed my name.

Then I put down my pen and felt pleased with my work. I wanted to show him that I was free; that he'd not ensnared my feelings at all. But as I put down my pen, my eyes looked sad again, because I could still see his eyes looking at me, and I couldn't forget the brown penetrating stare. What did it mean?

Then I crossed out my letter and began another one.

'Dear Juan Carlos, I want you so much" I wrote. "I can't stop thinking about you. I am just writing to give you my address in case you want to keep in touch. Thank you again for the lovely night.'

I signed my name. It came to my mind, 'Would he know who I was?' Did I ever tell him my name? I couldn't remember whether I had told him, and if he had ever used my name.

Folding the letter, I put it inside an envelope and wrote 'Juan Carlos: El Hombre De Oro' on the front of it followed by the address of the hotel.

That night the air was balmy and though a stream of night air filtered in between the open window I had sat up to breath. I sat on the edge of the bed and put my head in my hands. I looked at the black windowpanes, closing me in from the silent garden, hearing my ceaseless hissing of Gerald's breath. The birds were ringing like bells and the sky was changing to navy blue and I'd been writing for hours.

I went out into the street with the letter in my hand. There was a blueing sky now, and a few lacy clouds. I crossed the road, and there wasn't a car or a person in the street, only the trees stood around between buildings along the pavements. I felt calm, seeing, above me, the leafy boughs of the trees dangling over Essex Road like mobiles and I dropped the letter into the red letterbox but when it had landed, with a paper whisper, deep inside the blackness of the box, I felt a nervous shiver, wondering all at once what deep creature I had ventured to rouse from its sleep.

Then a feeling of relief lifted me up. Finally I could sleep. The red pillar-box with its coat of shining red glass paint had swallowed it with satisfaction.

Each morning I went downstairs to collect the post. I was keen to look at all stamps to see if there was a Spanish one.

But having scooped up the letters, there was nothing from Spain. I let my arms flop down and closed my eyes, as if I felt pain. I believed it was my own head and my own imaginings that I'd been in love with and not him. I pictured him not having a clue about how magical it was - not having a clue, not finding me important at all.

The city was full of interesting things and I went for walks to try and forget him.

The air was green and the sun was like water lily leaves, mottling the pavement below. The trees above sparkled - like water. Their petals were like insect wings - flickering like flames and I stopped on the pavement to watch them while the pigeons stood like Chinese Emperors with long cloaks. I noticed a squirrel watching me and could not take my eyes off that squirrel. I sat there, for maybe an hour, watching it, lurching around the tree so that I could see its eyes. The squirrel had the finest brown eyes. They were so good-humoured, and yet so deep, quiet and kind... so like Juan Carlos's eyes had been.

'Have you come to visit me in the form of a squirrel?' I said, hopefully. I heard the noise of it breaking nuts and felt envious of its simple life. I wanted to be as small as it, break nuts with it. His mouth flickered as he chewed and then I heard the little thud where he'd chucked away a shell. He was curious of me too. He stayed near by and it was the longing in his eyes (nut hunger, perhaps) or perhaps it is the longing of companionship that I saw, which reminded me of Juan Carlos.

I thought only of my Gold Man. He was racking me to pieces. I went outside and I looked up with big longing eyes at the sky. The cars were a quiet, metal that I was afraid to touch in case they screamed their alarms. I felt the heat of day, still radiating from the metal. Smelt the rubber of the tyres. The sky was a pure milk, so perfectly dark and above I watched the cawing of black ravens. I noticed how their shining black feathers were so much like Juan Carlos's hair.

I decided to inform myself more about sex.
"What's a one night stand?" I asked my friend Richard discretely one evening.

"Well a one night stand, you walk away from it and forget it for good" he said, shrugging simply. I was quiet as I considered this. "And a one night stand you often regret it...once you no longer fancy them... once you've had the sex and that's all you wanted from them"

"What do you mean?" I said. I pictured my gold man and his eyelids, quick to blink and they were plump, large - with black fringe of hair.

"Have you never had a one night stand?" he said, looking at me in disbelief.

"No, I kissed a few men before Gerald" I muttered quietly.

"Well I don't sleep with English women anymore," he continued.

"Why?" I asked

"They don't know what to do in bed. They just lie there and think of England. It's like fucking the Dartford Tunnel, there's no friction especially with the ones with wide hips. I prefer Thai women. They treat sex like gymnastics and they make me feel like I'm big because their holes aren't as sagging and wet,"

I listened attentively and then felt downcast. Was that why Juan Carlos hadn't written because I was a Dartford Tunnel?

Was that what I was to Juan Carlos: a one nightstand - and not very good? I felt stupid.

In secret moments I found myself flexing my cervix – worried that I too was a Dartford Tunnel. Had he lay on his back: not because he was fifty and tired, but because I had a floppy cervix and he couldn't create friction? He had given up. That was why he let me go so easily, without even asking for my address. That was why he let his penis flop on his belly - slapping the tummy with a lazy, tired flap, why he hadn't touched me when I was touching him. Why none of my little bed tricks had pleased him. And why he didn't rush after me for my address.... and I thought he was afraid I would reject him! So I sent him my address! What a fool I was - at least he'll feel flattered, and also afraid I might pursue him further.

I imagined myself in sunglasses, and sexy, black clothes, stalking by with Gerald on my arm - sexually happy - like a fluttery bird, Gerald cocksure and him just watching and feeling morose and realising it wasn't such an easy pull after all.

Another day came and I got up as usual and went for the post. The letters were lit by a streak of morning sunlight. There were three letters lying on the doormat, one white, and two brown envelopes. But there was nothing from him and I felt a pain slither through me when there was no letter. I told myself it had just been a fuck, a quick fuck, and told myself not to love him. He was just a hunter and he'd killed me with all the rest he ensnared. I saw the dead look in his eyes, the lazy look, where I was no longer alive for him to bother strangling.

"Down getting the post again?" Gerald said. He was smoking in bed and releasing a trail of silver smoke. He stubbed his cigarette out on a plate of toast crumbs and grinned at me. His yellowed teeth seemed glazed as he kissed me noisily near my earlobe.

But when Gerald opened a bottle of wine later, I drank the wine as if it was water, glass after glass. Then I went outside. The trees had green branches shaped like palm trees and they were all wild and raving like the heads of a dinosaur. Later that night they rustled and the roadway was a river of sweet, leafy smelling air and the sky was soft to my eyes, a bit cross-eyed, and my mouth was numb. I sat on the pavement, hidden by parked cars, drunk on red wine. I smelt of its vinegar. Little red stains were on either side of my mouth.

I looked up with big longing eyes at the sky. I heard the sigh of the treetops. The hot blue night sky, hot as my longing heart. I was all alone wanting Juan Carlos. I was haunted by things about him, and frightened that he wouldn't get out of my head, and that I'd only be free when I saw him and found out that he didn't want me. But then I was frightened of being honest and then losing him. Why did he happen? Why did I have to go and sleep with him? I had looked in books that might have answers, and found nothing.

I found myself in Covent Garden, the land of mime artists. The sun decided to dazzle the place - and all the buildings went vanilla coloured and the road went silver. I ran along the road, so that the wind lifted up my hair, making it light as confetti. The Covent Garden cobblestones were shining like mother of pearl, the sound of people's shoes on the cobbles, sounded like golf balls being putted. The daylight was bright, blazing the pavement and the shadows lay on them, deep grey and sharp edged.

Then all at once, I saw a mime artist. It stood on a pedestal. It was covered in silver greaseproof paint, and at once I smiled, my face lit up, as if I had seen an old friend. I went straight over to it, weaving quickly through the people, almost knocking them, impatient to get to it. I stopped, in front of it. It was a silver robot. It had a tin colander for a hat and big silver gloves and silver greaseproof paint smeared into its skin.

But its eyes were icy blue, indifferent - almost angry, and I watched them, longingly, waiting in front of them. I could see its nose, which was arched, and its lips so thin, like rolled up cigarettes, and eventually the eyes looked at me, but they flicked past me, as if I had left no trace or impression. They seemed dull, cold eyes that glanced past me as if I weren't even there. I felt a stab of disappointment, and looked sorrowful and devastated. I looked drably at the robot for a while, before stepping back.

Then, somewhere I could hear a pounding noise, rhythmic and noisy and sitting in front of the church, there was another artist, playing a drum. I wandered over to him and stood watching his eyes. He had brown eyes, but they seemed so gormless to me. I wanted him to be boring, to have no charisma in his eyes: so that I knew only Juan Carlos had it. His eyes were like chocolate buttons and his face was all whitened. I imagined our faces meeting, kissing and being smeared with the white face paint, but it was so dull an idea. There seemed a futility in getting his white smudges on my lips. The drummer seemed depressed, nodding his head sulkily and hitting the drum as if angry, his lips pouted sulkily.

One night Gerald had gone out and I was alone in the flat. It was a hot blue night sky, hot as my longing heart and all I was wanting was Juan Carlos.

Suddenly I went to the drawer and pulled it open. I took out his business card. Sharp rays of sunlight hit me like arrows and hurried into the living room bookcase.

In front of me, on the business card was the telephone number.

I opened the Spanish dictionary and flicked through the tussle of pages, writing down some words.

Then I went to the phone. I dialled the code for Spain. Then I dialled the hotel.

My hand was shaking and my skin was getting hot and damp. I waited, as a long dialling tone happened for a while - the long tone on the continent - then, there was a soft voice. My heart was beating faster and I heard again the sacred air I'd breathed in with him.
"Buenos Dias. Hotel Alcapora. Como le piedo ayudar hoy?" His voice was grainy, low, flat and bored. Drearily he spoke then he waited for my reply.
"El hombre Doray" I said "El hombre Doray" Then there was silence.
"Eh?" I heard. It was a quick, irritated voice.
It was hard to mould my gums around the words. My lips were sloppy, like spaghetti. I tasted only acrid red wine. The wine had made my body flop. Made my mouth numb. I could only say his name.
I collected my words, repeated.
"El hombre d'Oray," I repeated
"Non, non" he said and the phone clicked.
The click pricked me like a pin. It went dead and he'd hung up. I looked surprised, stunned, then hurt and I stood up, tears in my eyes.

One day my brother called and asked me out I put on my coat.
"Where are you going?" Gerald asked suspiciously.
"To meet my brother"
"But you have agreed to be with me!" he said.
"It's just for a quick drink. I haven't seen him for ages."
"You're not going," he said. His tone made me feel dismal. He put his key in the lock and bolted me up in the flat. He stood in front of the door, staring at me.
The breeze blew freely, but I was locked inside and he wouldn't let me go outside. I looked at the lock. Gerald's arms waited on either side of his waist, on the ready, in case I should try and get past him, but I sat on the bed, for I just didn't want to try anymore.
The red numbers on the digital clock were throbbing and throbbing like the blood in my veins and I saw them flashing the time I was supposed to meet my brother.
"At least let me call my brother to say I can't come?" but he stood in front of the phone." I don't want to argue. It's late," I murmured.
"Just like you to act as if nothing's wrong"
I went to the bed and lay down as if tired and closed my eyes
"Don't just get into bed and sleep as if nothing has happened!" he cried. He was hovering at the side of the bed and his hair was stuck up and his eyes were metallic and fixed on me. He was almost at my heal. He was watching me fixedly.
"Please don't," I said. I closed my eyes and thought of my gold man.

Suddenly I felt something wet land on my face. I felt the spit land on my eyelids. It was heavy and wiped it off onto the duvet cover. My face was all damp. It seemed sticky, like the shiny surface of a sugarcoated bun. He crouched in the dim light of the bedroom bulb, so his face could be level with my face and watched me closely, as if he was examining all that was wrong with me. I kept my eyes closed.

"So you think you can just sleep, as if nothing's happened?" he repeated. I lay like a corpse. I didn't speak or even open my eyes. He spat again, pelting my face, every few seconds. The pelting of the spit came every few seconds, again and again, until my face was soaked in his spit. He didn't speak at all, just spat and kept spitting.

I lay in the silent night, hearing the bullet like click of his lips as the minutes passed. Again and again he spat, so that my face was soaked in the wet splats. They dripped down my cheeks and over my nose, down my chin and landed on the sheets below.

Outside it was very dark. All the other buildings were in darkness and peace, except for our room, which blazed in a dim, tired urine yellow light. I waited and waited, feeling the night burn on, feeling time go by, waiting in the slow time, thinking of the soft brown gaze of Juan Carlos, and feeling how his eyes looked at me, imagining them loving me while all the time my face was studded with spit.

After a long time, it seemed, half an hour, an hour, my face and hair drenched, Gerald seemed to have got bored of it. He stood up, and I heard his footsteps leave the room. He walked along the corridor and I heard him go into the kitchen. I could smell the rancid scent of cigarette smoke, creeping down the corridor.

When he was gone, I crept quietly to the bathroom and bathed my face in water from the sink. The water was gentle and soothing and I dabbed it over my skin as if my face was wounded, before getting back into bed.

I woke up one morning and find Gerald is sitting on the other side of the bed, reading my journal. He was looking at me, with disbelief as if he really can't grasp it.
"You slept with some man on a street in Spain" he said
"It was just sex" I said.
"Why?" he said, his jaw hanging down.
"It was just the once," I said.

After Gerald had read my journal, I moved out of our comfortable Islington flat.
Then, after a couple of weeks, Gerald rang me and said he would have me back to live with him again.
"But I was unfaithful to you" I said
"Well it was just a one off wasn't it?" he said.
I thought about our comfortable flat and having him to love me as I had never lived alone before. It was cold and lonely. The bedsit room was only three metres by three metres near Paddington Station. It was like the inside of a sugar cube. It smelt of whitewash. It had a long thin window, almost as thin as the slit window of a castle and a nice view of a garden, in which there were squirrels, which had rugged hill backs. There was a lamp, flooding a tender, gold light over my desk, and on the bed, the white sprawl of bed linen, waiting to bandage me up in sleep, like I was an Egyptian king.
I enjoyed my first day there. I loved the light, all the garden light, bright on the walls, like milk, and Gerald's shadow wasn't breaking into it. My friend Richard helped me move in. when I clicked on my new kettle, it hissed and gurgled. The kitchen was all my own, like a little girl's play kitchen, cute and small, in which I could prepare tasty, healthy little meals
We dropped lacy teabags into two mugs.
"It reminds me of those bedsits in 'Up the Junction' - those places Yorkshire girls went to when they left home for London" Richard said.

But when he had finished his tea and had gone I was alone again. The fridge buzzed, like an electric razor and, although I struggled to eat, for I struggled to be natural, because I was afraid, all the time, of being alone and this voice inside my kept saying "You will go mad living alone."

Gerald had been my calm home, and for nine years, my family, keeping me sane, and, all of a sudden, he wasn't there anymore, and my secure life had suffered an earthquake. I wasn't sure I liked the silence. I felt shocked, beginning to realise that Gerald wasn't there. He wasn't going to lie next to me, and sometimes I felt like bursting into tears for no reason and in the morning, when I woke up, my stomach was all stiff, like a cheeseboard, and I felt all seized up and hyper, unable to relax.

I went to drink a glass of water, taking the sips in really slowly, hoping that my stomach would go soft, but it just wouldn't and I ended up feeling a tense frenzy and worried that the only person who could calm me down was Gerald.

When I first moved into the little bedsit room I switched on the television. "Mrs Simpson had anorexia," said the voice in the television, "She suffered from it in her early life. 'How do you keep your beauty?' she was asked. She answered: 'I suppose happiness makes you beautiful'" she said.

I froze with fear, turning off the television immediately, assuming I would be unhappy and become ugly. Then I noticed a large brown stain had soaked its way through from upstairs and I wondered whether it was tea. I could see a couple of little brown beetles busy crossing the ceiling, with long antennae. The window seemed to wobble about, and I wondered if the previous occupant had made LSD in the room and that I was hallucinating.

There was a bass drum pounding from one of the other rooms, and I touched the brillo pad, dirty blue of the carpet. More of the little insects were crawling over the wall, over my desk. Some were large with great brown shell-like backs and their antennas twitched. The heater creaked in the chill autumn air. Some of them walked over my pillow. The white sky was chill, there was no yellow warmth in the garden, only flat, cold light and I looked at my face in the mirror.

The eyes were pale, blue, and dull, and I had black eye lashes and black eyebrows and my eyes looked lost and scared. I sat down on the bed and stared ahead of me. All day the trees had been sprayed in rain. The garden was soaking. I felt so empty, and I didn't want to go outside ever again. I just wanted to close my eyes and sleep. The night would come and my bulb would burn - shining on me until I was a microscopic view of loneliness.

I knew Gerald waited. He was the only man who had ever loved me. Without him I worried I would become a bum. Give up. Have cockroaches fill the place. Fall apart. I decided I would have no will to go on. No care. My electric metre would run out of coins. I'd get pimples all over my back. I was feeling them rise up on my forehead already from the worry. The adverts beside the escalators would go past, their efforts to sell saying 'pointless, pointless, pointless.' Their colours would become more garish and people's faces, face after face, would look numb and empty, just like life really was, how it had been in my lonely life before Gerald.

Grief was on my face, like someone who was bereaved and I lay down on the bed with agony in my heart. I had felt love but it had not been real. Love was not real. Love did not exist. I felt so foolish and worried that I was some kind of mad Don Quixote, trying to reach something that was not real.

Here was Gerald in the flesh who said he loved me and wanted me and I panicked and wondered what was wrong with me for dithering. No clear answer had come. Instead the cockroaches poured in from the holes in the floorboards and I was alone night and day. I worried that if I stayed there forever I would go mad from the loneliness.

So when Gerald rang and asked me on a date, I said yes at once. I met him in Highgate woods. I was pleased to see him and we acted like boyfriend and girlfriend, holding hands. We went to a Shamanist theatre production in Highgate Woods. The Shamans were coated in green greasepaint from head to foot and wore little ragged robes. One shaman introduced it said:
"It's good to get the kids out - away from TV and video games"
All the characters spent about five whole minutes frozen still. They were so still that the audience started shuffling about looking bored. I thought 'I bet the kids are wishing they'd stayed at home to watch their video games'. The shamans said they liked to feel 'at one' with nature. They moved like trees and felt sympathy with everything and were kind to everything.
At the end the characters (who were called fairies) ran and hid in the woods. All these tiny children went to look for them.
"There's a present," said the narrator "if you find it,"
These children really ran. When they found their present, they were holding a few green leaves. These kids looked at the leaves trying not to frown their disappointment.
You could tell they were expecting sweets or some plastic toy or something. When the shamans said:

"Go and look at the treasure" lots of kids went under the bushes. There were fairies under there too. I looked to see if the parents looked concerned about the safety of their kids under a bush with a total stranger and I was just wondering what the treasure would be when I found myself all embarrassed, because I was lured by a fairy under the bush.
"No, no, it's ok" I said, trying to get away. I wondered how to react to this fairy. She said
"Look at the treasure." and in the ground there was a mirror. I could see my forehead, her face and the sky.
"What do you see?" she asked.
"The top of my head," I replied.
"What's the most important thing you can see?" I was going to say, "You" just to please her, but I said "the sky" because I didn't want to say "Me" and be vain. "Is that what I'm supposed to say?" I added. She shrugged.
"You can say what you want. But I would say 'me' and I would think for you it was 'you' and look again at yourself: see how you've got sparkles in your eyes? Remember those, when everything is dark for you, remember those sparkles in your eyes"

Then Gerald said:
"I know that gold man was a womaniser, but I'll have you back. I would go around the world for you... I TRULY love you"
Then I heard his voice in the answer machine, inviting me back. He told me I could have my wardrobe back, and everything could go back to normal. He told me I could go and live with him again in our cosy, secure, box-like flat.

I didn't move. I folded back the shutter and saw the speckles of pink and white blossom and felt the cool air flushing against my face. It was a very gold day. The window was like a mouth and the air its breath. I saw how the milk white sky swam above the long green haired garden and how, up in the tree, were two wood pigeons, perched on a branch, fanning out their tails all regal seeming, like two Elizabethan queens.

There was a sound of hushing, without intermission as if nature was a tired dragon, collapsing down and breathing its honey filled mellifluous breath into my face. I leant my face a little further out of the window and found that the grass had turned to satin, sparkling like green aluminium foil, making the flowers look like little lights with different coloured shades.

The sun fell over the gardens and shone its way into the bedsit, lighting up my greasy eyelids like hot soup. I felt it ooze over me and gently the chiffon curtain drifted too and fro angelically. I crawled over my bed to sit at the window and watch the garden. The trees reached up to the sky with snake-like, buckled bark and so burdened with green leaves they sagged. The pink and huge blossoms on the ends of the branches had fallen onto the lawn and paled it white. I saw the grey white sky and the garden, with its long green hair, once shaved and now the hair was growing back, spilling and fountaining.

The garden rasped and hissed like a dying creature breathing its last as if stabbed by a matador and now it seemed to be an underwater sea, a drowned jungle of weird shaped plants, dome-shaped and fountain shaped swilling into the walls of my mind and dissolving them away and I continued to sit alone at the window.

I envied all the couples who had found someone who they loved; I kept my elbows on the window. Determined I should be that way too, and though perhaps soppy to think it, I felt the wheels, the great water wheels of feeling, of experience would turn, and I would be spun like butter until I was pure, creamy and ready for love, for I felt the wheels would turn and I would be lead.

The End

Printed in Great Britain
by Amazon